# THE
# KINGDOM

# THE
# KINGDOM

by

## Steven Szmyt

Mill City Press, Maitland, FL

Mill City Press, Inc.
2301 Lucien Way #415
Maitland, FL 32751
407.339.4217
www.millcitypublishing.com

ISBN-13: 978-1-63505-296-1
LCCN: 2016910968
Edited by: W. Todd Abernathy

Printed in the United States of America

for Kitty and Mom for your support
and
Sydney, Sammy and Stacey for
your encouragement

# CONTENTS

# ACKNOWLEDGMENTS

I would like to thank Todd Abernathy, Ryan Qualls,
Rebecca Mahoney for all their creative input.
And especially
Wendie Appel
for helping this ship set sail.

# ARUSHA, TANZANIA

A dusty white Range Rover winds down the sandy streets of the busy Tanzanian town known as Arusha. The streets are bustling with all manner of vehicles. The air is thick with the smell of diesel. Run down and battered taxis sit at every intersection. Overloaded trucks struggle under the weight of their loads. Motorcycles and scooters dart between the slower moving vans and cargo trucks.

The streets are littered with potholes, which have clearly taken their toll on the vehicles that drive them. Roads like these would never pass US standards. This is just the first act of a circus that takes place every morning in Arusha. Soon businesses will display their wares and await the arrival of eager shoppers.

The sidewalks are also busy. Stray dogs skitter up and down alleys looking for food. Groups of young girls dressed in their uniforms make their way to school. Frantic men hustle all around, loading and unloading their deliveries to various shops and warehouses.

Shop owners wait outside for their first customers to arrive. Some sit in the shade that is provided by the dilapidated awnings that hang above their storefronts. As most shops don't have air conditioning, this is an early morning treat that allows them to stay cool in the arid conditions.

A majority of the buildings the Range Rover pass are no bigger than two stories. They are all faded white from the oppressive African sun. Layers of dust and sand have settled along their windowsills and awnings. A maze of telephone and electrical wires dangle above the streets, connecting all the buildings to one another like a giant spider web.

It is late in the morning and already the hot climate is starting to take its affect on the passengers inside the vehicle. Their shirts show signs of perspiration under their arms as they wipe sweat from their faces with their sleeves and handkerchiefs.

The four Americans inside the rented Rover are longtime friends who met in their time at Texas A&M. Now in their mid-forties, they get together several times a year to travel and revel in the past. One of them, Dwight, the most obnoxious in the group, starts the morning's conversation with some highlights of his observations.

"Ya know, I don't understand these people. I don't think they know how good they have it here. The weather is beautiful here every day and aside from an infrequent lion attack here and there, they have no natural disasters. This could be the next Vegas with the right investors."

The other three quietly chuckle and nod their heads in agreement.

"Seriously," he continues, "look at what they've done in Dubai with all the new golf courses, hotels and shopping. They made a paradise out of sand.

These people have found paradise but instead, they choose to live like this, such a waste."

Phil, who is sitting next to Dwight and is on the heavier side, is mainly included in the group's outings because of his sense of humor. He isn't as wealthy or athletically gifted as the others but his quick wit is a welcome break from the constant "mine is bigger than yours" sparring that the other three constantly indulge in.

"Well, I guess they don't call them third world nations unless there's a reason," Phil responds.

They all laugh.

Dwight continues, "By the way Richard, I still don't completely understand why you cancelled our hunting trip. We'd planned this for months and then you just suddenly at the last minute cancel it?"

Richard is the self-proclaimed leader of the group. He is the type of person who is always looking for something bigger and better. He is athletically built and was once the star college quarterback of the group's alma mater. He craves attention and he demands the best in any activity he undertakes. This is so that he is always able to one up someone in a conversation. His broad chest is overshadowed only by his loud Texas voice.

"Because, my friend, I found something a little more to our level of expertise."

"Oh yeah? Well, for what we're spending, it had better be," replies Dwight.

"Don't worry, you won't be disappointed," Richard responds.

After a twenty-minute journey from their hotel, Richard squints through the dusty windshield and finally spots his destination.

"Ah, here we are. This is the place gents."

He pulls up to a small two-story building with flaking white paint. The Rover comes to a stop alongside a rickety wooden cart that is overloaded with broken furniture and TVs. Hitched up to the cart is a huge ox. As the dust kicked up from the Rover settles, a sign painted across the large window begins to appear. The faded red lettering reads "<u>The Geti Plains:</u> The Ultimate in Wildlife Hunting Trips."

"Hey Richard, just because it says it, doesn't mean it's true," Phil snickers.

"Will you guys quit your gripin'. I'm tellin' ya, you're not going to believe what we're in for."

Dwight turns to get out of the car when he is startled to see the ox face to face with him in his open window.

"Geyaaah!" he shouts. "Shoo, go away you," gesturing the cow away with his hand. The others laugh at Dwight's predicament and exit the vehicle.

They follow one another into the shop led by Richard. As the door swings open, it strikes a small, antiquated bell that is hanging above the door. Its jingle alerts the man behind the counter to the group's arrival. He is a smallish, dark skinned man who hunches slightly and is clearly not African. Judging from his short stature and his accent, Richard surmises correctly that he is from India.

The man is wearing a loose fitting white cotton outfit with an elegant purple vest. A red fez adorns the top of his head. The name-tag on his vest reads, "Reginald" and it quickly becomes apparent to the four men that he has a habit of not looking at whom he is speaking. His mangy dark hair hangs across parts of his face as he nervously looks from side to side.

Richard steps up to the counter leading with his chest and speaks in his boisterous Texan draw.

"Good morning my good man, we are four expert hunters in search of the hunt. I'm led to believe this is the establishment to go for the ultimate hunting experience."

The other three roll their eyes and grin at one another.

Reginald replies in a whiny morbid tone. "Well, we have hunting trips that leave every morning at 6."

Richard is taken back by Reginald's prompt response. However, this clearly wasn't the answer he wanted to hear.

"Yes, I am aware of that fact, my good man, but I don't think you understand me. I was led to believe that this establishment offers another entirely *different* hunting experience and that is why we are here."

Unamused by Richard's belittling tone, Reginald's attitude quickly changes. He looks over his shoulder at the open doorway behind him, as if checking for something. He then quickly turns and looks directly at Richard for the first time during their brief conversation. Staring coldly into Richard's eyes, Reginald quietly states, "Are you sure?"

Not used to being questioned, especially by such a timid person, Richard is rendered speechless by the remark. His friends, however, are finding great amusement in it.

An uncomfortable silence fills the room until a tall well-kept man with dark hair and confidant eyes appears in the doorway behind Reginald. The hanging beads that separate the two rooms slide over his shoulders then quickly drop off as he passes through the opening. When he takes his place beside Reggie on the counter, his presence causes the others to take a slight step back. There is an aura about him that suggests power that makes them uneasy.

He, like Reginald, is also wearing a loose fitting white cotton outfit but without the vest. The man looks down at Reginald for a brief second. Reginald is again averting his eyes, staring away from the man down at the floor. The newcomer slowly turns his head toward the men. With a calm and pleasant smile, he introduces himself.

"Good morning gentlemen, my name is Beauregard Ramses. Perhaps I can be of service?"

His accent is clearly British, which again startles Richard, who wasn't expecting to converse with someone so well spoken.

"Well, yeah, as I was asking-" he looks at Reginald's name-tag again, "Reggie here. I heard about this special night expedition that you guys offer."

Beauregard gives Richard a once over then briefly looks at the ceiling as if pondering a thought. He slowly lowers his head back down, once again making eye contact with Richard. He proudly responds to the request.

"Yes, there is an exclusive expedition, one that only *we* offer."

Tom, the last member of the party and generally the quieter of the quartet steps up to the counter.

"Would you mind explaining what this special expedition is," he asks.

Beauregard grins at the men in the room to lighten the mood.

"Ah, yes, my apologies. It is an all-inclusive night hunting expedition. And gentlemen, when I say all-inclusive, I mean we take care of everything for you; food, travel and lodging. You don't have to lift a finger, that is, except to shoot. It is, gentleman, the ultimate hunting safari. However, due to the permits that we have arranged with the local authorities and the Tanzanian government, the trip comes at a premium price. There is also quite a bit of manpower needed to undertake such a trip-"

Richard interrupts, "That, Mr. Beauregard, will not be a problem. I think I can speak for us all, when I say," as he looks to his friends for agreement, "we are ready when you are."

"Well, very well then," Beauregard responds as he looks down to Reginald.

"Reginald, would you please start the paperwork for these fine men?"

"Yes sir," Reginald whimpers.

Beauregard looks back to the men and states, "Gentlemen, I leave you in the capable hands of my assistant. Be prepared, you leave at sunset tonight."

Beauregard turns and walks into the back room, his calming yet shark like smile never fading as he disappears back through the beads.

It is just past sunset and two older style Land Cruisers bounce their way through the African bush. Richard and Dwight are in the lead vehicle scanning the plain for any sign of what they believe they will be hunting. They both have been on numerous hunting trips together over the past several years but they relish this unique opportunity.

Tom and Phil are in the second truck quietly wondering how they will do on this, their first hunting trip. They are both familiar with firing guns but never in anger at a live animal.

The night is comfortable and warm but the parched air is still affecting the four travelers, causing them to drink more frequently to moisten their throats. Though the sun has only just set, the darkness of night is quickly spreading across the barren grassland.

The trucks have both headlights and numerous overhead spotlights focused on the road ahead. After a rough two hours of driving, the two Toyotas finally creep to a stop. Once the engines are silenced, the two now seemingly anxious drivers roll up their windows.

Reginald, who is driving the lead truck, turns and looks over to Richard.

"We are here, sir. Time to get ready. The creatures should come through this area within the next couple of hours."

The two hunters step out of their vehicle and head to the back of their truck. Tom and Phil observe and follow suit. They all start to loosen tie down straps so they can unload their bags. Once finished, they can start preparing their gear. Phil finds it curious that neither Reggie nor the other driver have left the vehicles to help.

"Eh Richard, what's up with them?" pointing to the drivers.

Richard looks over his shoulder lowering his brow in puzzlement.

"Don't know. We're big boys though, we can handle this ourselves."

"Thought this was all inclusive?" Phil mutters to Tom.

Tom shakes his head and smirks back at him.

Once settled, they climb up on top of their respective vehicles to wait. For the next 45 minutes, the hunters take respite listening to the numerous sounds in this primitive land. Sounds like the deep roar of distant lions to the repetitive yelping of nearby hyenas. Noticeably, the air goes silent. Reginald and the other driver look all around and both slide down low in their seats. The men, clutching their rifles, all look around in bewilderment, not one of them daring to make a sound. Seconds turn to minutes and still not a sound except for the swaying of grass blowing in the night breeze. The night sky is remarkably clear and infinite. Unfortunately, because of the adrenaline boost the men are feeling, the awe-inspiring view of the stars from this serene grassland goes unnoticed.

Then off in the distance, a sound breaks the silence. A sound that is not native to this part of the world. It is a howl. The unmistakable howl of a wolf.

Richard's eyes open wide with excitement. "Did you hear that?"

"Yeah," responds Dwight. "Is that what I think it is?"

Tom looks at Phil awkwardly. "There aren't wolves in Africa, are there?"

"No, there aren't."

"Well what the hell was that?"

"Sounded like-" he pauses, "a wolf."

Phil whispers over to the other truck, "Richard, Dwight, what's going on?"

"Shhh, I'm not sure but I am sure you might be the first person I know to bag a wolf in Africa. Now be quiet and put on your goggles."

Stunned and amazed, the hunters prepare to hunt what in their mind is an astounding find, a wolf pack in the Serengeti Plain.

Reginald, who is the coordinator of the trip, looks around nervously. He rolls his window down a little and through the small opening, urges the hunters to be on alert.

"Now be careful. They know we are here."

"You know about these wolves?" Richard asks.

"Yes, very rare, now pay attention."

He rolls up his window completely.

More and more howls can now be heard. The tall blades of grass split apart like a boat cutting through water as the creatures close in on the vehicles. Through their night vision goggles, the hunters catch glimpses of the animals running about in the distance. Their eyes shine bright and then disappear amidst the dense grass. The second driver, sweating and nervous, stares wide-eyed out the windows of his vehicle. Unsure of what will happen next, he makes sure all the windows in his vehicle are rolled up and the doors are all locked.

The two less experienced hunters, Tom and Phil, do their best to find a target, take aim and fire. They squeeze their triggers and the blasts from their guns cause the creatures to scatter. They reload, aim, and fire again. They look to one another and are surprised to realize that they haven't hit anything. Easily frustrated, Phil advances another bullet into the chamber, takes aim and fires. The shot misses again.

"Did we get one?" Tom yells to the other truck.

Dwight yells back, "I don't think so, take your time and aim."

"Take my time and aim? What the hell does he think we're doing?" Tom mutters to Phil.

Richard fires off a round.

"Damn, I missed. These things are quick," he barks to Dwight.

Dwight and Richard each fire off another round.

Richard pulls the armature back, then forward, chambering another round in his rifle.

"What the hell? I'm only able to see bits of them then they're gone," he shouts irritated.

The hunters can hear growls and barking as the wolves now coordinate their advance.

All four men fire quicker and more sporadically, still missing shot after shot. Beginning to get a little unnerved, Dwight defiantly jumps down from the roof of the Rover to pursue the wolves on foot. Reginald sees this and quickly alerts the hunter to stay with the vehicle.

"What are you crazy? Get back to the truck!"

The hunters continue to see wolves roaming through the grass, circling their position. They take a few more shots but miss. The pack continues to work their way closer and closer to the vehicles.

"Screw this, I'm going down with Dwight," shouts Tom.

"Yeah, I'm with ya on that."

Both Tom and Phil jump down off the truck to get closer to their prey. Dwight, who is now twenty yards from the vehicle, hears a sudden rustling in the grass beside him. He quickly turns to encounter one of the wolves leaping from the bush up at him. The wolf's two front paws dig hard into his chest knocking him off his feet. His arms fling back desperately trying to catch his fall as his rifle goes sailing into the night sky. He hits the ground hard but before he can react, two other wolves lunge in with ferocity. One attacks and bites deep into Dwight's shoulder while the other latches onto his opposite arm. He lets out a childlike shriek. With a firm hold, they quickly drag Dwight away screaming into the grass.

Richard, watching through his scope in horror, fires a shot to help his friend but again misses his target. He watches as several more wolves converge on his friend. In a matter of seconds, Dwight's garbled screams are silenced far off in the darkness.

Tom and Phil, who had briefly started to run after their fallen comrade, stop and promptly re-evaluate their situation.

"Shit man, I think Dwight's dead."

"Oh man, I didn't sign up for this shit." Phil utters nervously.

"Neither did I. Let's get back to the fucking truck," shouts Tom.

The two men turn and sprint back toward the vehicles.

"Ooof!"

Out of nowhere, Phil is hit hard from his blind side by something large, knocking him to the ground and scattering all his gear everywhere. He winds up lying on his side, leaning on one elbow and holding his head with his other hand, trying to gather his senses.

Tom stops and looks back for his missing partner. "Phil?!? You ok?"

He scans the area but sees nothing through the swaying field.

"Phil, where are you?" he yells again.

"I'm over here," waving his arm in the air. "I ran into something. I'm ok."

"You ran into something? Phil, there isn't anything here to run into!" Tom shouts back.

Richard, increasingly frustrated by his inability to kill anything, is also getting concerned about the safety of his friends.

"Get back here you guys! You're too far from the trucks. Did you not just see what happened to Dwight?" Feeling around on his hands and knees for his night vision goggles, Phil is alerted to the sound of something big slowly approaching him. He looks up to witness a huge creature, walking upright, emerging from the grass. Unable to see much in the dark, he can only make out what looks to be dark, matted fur covering the beast with a long protruding snout glistening with razor sharp teeth. The creature hovers over Phil who is frozen with fear. It emits a low snarl as it bares its teeth in the fallen hunter's face.

Phil whimpers, "What the -" only to be silenced with a quick strike to his head delivered from the creature's massive claw. Phil's body goes limp and slumps to the ground.

Richard is watching in horror and amazement as he sees another one of the creatures emerge from the grass near his friend's body. Two more wolves join in and start gorging themselves on Phil's flesh.

Richard yells to Reggie.

"Reggie, what the hell are those things?"

"This is the ultimate hunting experience you asked for sir," Reggie whispers to himself as he sinks deeper into his seat.

Tom, who has stumbled upon his fallen friend being devoured by these unexplained phenomenon, drops his gun and sprints back towards the trucks. He quickly becomes panicked and screams in distress.

"Help me Richard, help me!"

Richard, now standing on the roof of the Land Cruiser, watches his friend running toward him. Frantically, he surveys the surrounding grass through his scope, trying to see if anything is chasing him. As before, he can only catch quick glimpses of movement but nothing to take aim at. He wipes the sweat on his face with his forearm and peers back into his scope.

In a quick flash of movement, a wolf bites the back of Tom's leg. He yells in pain as another leaps at him from the front, buckling him to the ground.

They pin him in the dirt, tearing at his body as he screams in agony.

"Richard! Help me!"

Richard can now clearly see two wolves through his scope. He takes aim at one of them and slowly squeezes the trigger.

"Now I gotcha," he whispers.

But before he fires, he hears a very low growl that sounds very, very close to him. His body feels hollow as if the blood has drained to his feet. Hair on the back of his neck bristles. A dark object rises up in front of him blocking his view through the scope.

"What the -?"

He lowers the rifle down from his face to witness one of the creatures silhouetted against the bright moonlit sky towering above him. Its enormous hand with menacing claws strikes down on Richard's head. The impact crushes his skull and his body drops limp on the roof of the truck.

Richard's body jerks several times, and then ceases all movement. The creature jumps to the ground and pulls the corpse down off the vehicle. A wolf runs over and drags it off into the grass where others are waiting.

The chaos and screams have all stopped. Once the creatures have had their share from the night's kill, they each slowly disappear back into the darkness. As it was earlier in the evening, there is again silence. For an area that is rich with life, it is eerily quiet. Not even the nighttime murmurs of distant lions can be heard.

Once more, the silence is broken by a single howl. At this, the two drivers start up the trucks, flick on their lights and proceed to drive away.

# THE PROFESSOR

I t is a crisp fall mid-October day in the quaint town of Elm Hills, NH. Most of the leaves have fallen but what is left of the tree line is basked in brilliant reds, oranges and yellows.

Although this is a college town, hiding alongside the roads and back streets there are many indications of money. Large colonials sit back away from the road while a select few corporates like the Gap and Banana Republic have maneuvered their way in along Main street. The charm of the town is made up of bookstores, cafes and restaurants.

A car passes by and a maelstrom of fallen leaves scatter in its wake. Professor Robert Caerwyn, who is originally from England, moved to this historic New England town about 15 years ago. He walks along the sidewalk through the center of town breathing in the cool air. Its freshness makes him smile. He has long enjoyed living in New England, especially here in New Hampshire, where there are but two simple mottos to live by; "If you don't like the weather, wait a minute," and "Wherever you need to go is always an hour away." The Professor knows the snow will be arriving soon, so he prefers to walk to work as often as he can before the cold sets in.

He is heading towards the college where he has taught history for the last twelve years. More cars pass by and the students no longer gather outside of the cafés. Instead, they've moved indoors where it's warm. The Professor shares the sidewalk with a group of students that are approaching him. In his customary manner, he smiles and greets them with a tip of his hat. He assumes that they are no doubt heading to the local café for a coffee and to take advantage of free Wi-Fi.

The Professor is in his early fifties and carries himself confidently. Walking tall with a sense of purpose, he is a man who demands your respect. His long tan overcoat only accentuates this persona. He has taught various history classes at the college but his area of expertise has focused on the history of religions, cults, and sects. Most anyone in town who knows him will say that he is one of the most respected teachers at the school and well-liked by much of the student body.

His dark hair hasn't grayed much, just a little on the sides. It is thick and well groomed. Ask any of the locals and no one will ever say they have seen the Professor unshaven.

As he walks, he catches sight of three nefarious young men on the opposite side of the street dressed in dirty jeans, hoodies, and leather jackets. They are standing in an alleyway next to the hardware store. He suspects they've been wearing the same clothes for days. He watches them as they flick their long disheveled hair away from their faces while cigarettes dangle from their lips. They joke and push at one another as one of them runs his nose along his sleeve.

The Professor has seen them around before and he knows they can be trouble. He would prefer not to draw their attention so he puts his head down and picks up his pace. Unfortunately for him they do see him. They know exactly who he is and take great pleasure in trying to humiliate this respected man.

"Hey, Mr. Braniac," the leader yells at the Professor.

"Yeah, hey you too good to teach us?"

He snaps his head towards them keeping his look stern as he continues on. Two of them pretend to blow kisses at the Professor as the leader of the three smirks and gives him a wink. Then, collectively, they turn and disappear back down the alleyway.

The Professor shakes his head in disgust as he looks up the road toward the school. His class begins in ten minutes. He'll be there in five.

Holy Trinity College began over 140 years ago and has graduated many great leaders of the modern time. Its stonework and colonial architecture make it one the most picturesque schools in New England. Because of his tenure, the Professor has been given the right to choose his classroom, which is located on the first floor of the main hall overlooking the rest of the campus.

Arriving at his classroom, he places his briefcase on his desk and hangs his coat on a hook by the door. Some students have arrived early and not to his surprise, the first person he acknowledges with a smile is Anne. He shouldn't be surprised. She's always early and always in the front row. He muses to himself that someday, something will happen and she'll be late or sitting in the back row. But she never is and never has in the three years the Professor has known her. She is on her cell phone speaking with her best friend Christina. She nervously acknowledges and smiles back at him. She then dives back to her notes that are laid out on her desk, all the while gabbing away on her cell.

Anne is a very modest girl, typically wearing outfits to obscure her natural beauty. She is thin with long, straight blond hair and she hardly ever wears makeup. She always dresses appropriately, normally wearing a blouse with a skirt or, like today, slacks. Her heavy fall coat is draped over the back of her seat from which she reaches for her glasses. She doesn't need glasses but wears them in class because they make her feel more confident. She also thinks they take focus away from her deep green eyes.

No one would ever describe her as being loud or outspoken, though she is always engaged in the classroom. She loves being a student and may not be very outgoing outside of class, but in class she shines. It is the one place she feels in control of her destiny.

Outside the Professor's classroom in the courtyard there is a large clock tower that sits atop the main building. It chimes every hour which to most signals when classes start. When it rings, the Professor starts to close the door but not before a few stragglers slip in before he closes it. The students know that when that door is closed, no one gets in and unless you are bleeding or dying you're not getting out.

Today's lecture is about paganism and its inevitable replacement, Christianity. The Professor begins his lecture as everyone simultaneously drops their eyes to their notebooks. His accent is British which many of his students enjoy because it's unusual to them. The others benefit from his superb pronunciation and prowess with manipulating the English language. Many times he amuses himself by using long forgotten words scattered throughout his diction and only when he starts to see the note taking slow down with confusion, will he pause to give definitions for those words. What brings him great pride is when he sees his students re-using those same words in their essays.

Now, pens are feverishly dashing across paper. He knows the material by heart and could easily recite from memory the whole hour but he knows he must pace himself so the students can keep up. While lecturing, he moves about the front of the room randomly jotting keywords on the chalkboard to emphasize their importance.

He leans back against his dark, antique desk watching Anne take notes. After graduation, she chose to continue on with her education and pursue her Master's degree, which is why she is once again hastily taking notes in one of the Professor's classes. She has a certain calmness with her note taking that brings him a sense of ease while he is lecturing. She is the type of student that makes teachers want to teach. Whenever the Professor asks questions, Anne always raises her hand to answer. If she doesn't understand something, she does everything she can to try to understand it. Anne is by far one of the best and brightest students the Professor can ever remember having and today he has something special to offer this gifted and dedicated young student.

When the bell finally rings signaling the end of class, the room erupts into organized chaos. As Anne reaches back for her coat, the Professor beckons her to his desk.

"Anne," he asks.

Startled, she looks up at him, "Yes Professor?" she replies.

He motions for her to approach his desk with his hand. She promptly gathers her things and does just that.

"What is it Professor," she asks?

"Anne, I was wondering if you would meet me at Durgin's for a cup of tea. I have a special assignment that I would like to discuss with you. What time are you through today?"

"My last class is done at 4:30."

"Is 4:45 ok," he asks. "Will that give you enough time to make it?"

"Yes, I can make that no problem."

"Good, 4:45 it is then. See you there. And Anne-"

"Yes, Professor?"

"Don't be late."

Anne stares at the Professor to see if he is joking. Clearly he isn't.

"No sir, I won't be."

She returns back to her desk and puts on her coat then shuffles her books into her bag. She exits the classroom with a hop in her step. She can only imagine what the Professor might ask of her, but she predicts that it undoubtedly will be significant to her.

Walking down the hall, she pulls out her phone and dials Christina.

Anne first met her their freshman year and they were roommates the following three years. Christina is the Ying to Anne's Yang. She is rough around the edges and defiantly mouthy.

There have been many times when Anne has had to step in between situations that Christina had created due to her quick tongue. She struggled throughout school and it was Anne who was instrumental in helping her get to graduation day. Christina, to her credit, has always tried to get Anne involved in things like parties, spring break trips, or going clubbing in Boston—all things that Anne would naturally feel uncomfortable in because she tends to be so introverted. Without each other, Christina probably wouldn't have graduated and Anne wouldn't have all the great experiences she now has. They both have a mutual respect for one another and a very strong friendship.

Christina grew up in Elm Hills and after graduation decided to stay because she likes the vibe of this small college community. Also, being a townie means she pretty much knows everyone, which gives her a certain degree of comfortableness. She took up a job waitressing at Durgin's and decided to stay.

The ringing stops and Christina answers Anne's call.

"What's up skinny?" Christina opens with.

"Don't call me that."

"Well, then put some meat on them bones."

"Whatever. Hey, guess what?"

"What?" Christina replies.

"The Professor asked me to meet him after school at Durgin's. He has some assignment or something he wants me to do. Isn't that exciting?"

There is a brief pause.

"You know he wants to fuck you, right?" Christina muses.

"Who?" Anne asks startled.

"Who do you think?"

"The Professor? Shut up, that's gross!"

"Yeah, then why else does he want to see you?"

"I don't know, I'm sure it's for some special project or report or something."

"Uh huh. The only special report he wants you to do is an under the covers investigative report on his Ivy league educated trouser snake."

"Christina, you are such a pig."

"Oh yeah, I'm the pig. I also have a little more experience than you. The only person you've ever been with is Rob. What you haven't learned yet is that all men are pigs, no matter what their age or what their stature. You mark my words, he wants you."

Anne reaches the end of the hallway where a doorway leads to another classroom.

"Look, Sweetie, who else is going to look out for you and keep all these scumbags away if not me?"

"I'll be fine. Not everyone is trying to have sex with me you know," Anne replies.

"That may be true because of the two of us," Christina retorts.

"Shut up, you're unbelievable."

"That's true. Anyhow, I gotta go. I'm on the clock. See you later at the shop?"

"Yeah, I'll see you there. What time do you get out?" Anne asks.

"Four thirty," replies Christina.

"Ok I'll see you there, bye"

"Ciao."

Anne swipes her finger across her phone and drops it into her coat pocket. The courtyard bell rings again and students scatter into various classrooms up and down the hall. Classroom doors close and the halls fall silent as Anne walks down the stairway.

# DURGIN'S

The Professor is sitting inside Durgin's at a small table in the corner of the café out of view from the outside. He likes this table because it is one of the few tables that allows for any sort of privacy. With one leg crossed over the other, he is sipping a cup of tea while sifting through the local newspaper.

Durgin's is a favorite of the campus community. It is the most popular coffee shop in town. Hanging on its bright yellow walls are pictures of famous people that have attended the college. A majority of them are well-known actors or political figures as well as some celebrated sports personalities. Most of them are now parents whose kids are, or will, be attending the school.

Anne walks in and sees Christina in her apron serving a customer. Christina looks up to see Anne giving her a smile and a wave. She returns the wave and points to the corner where the Professor is sitting. Anne looks in that direction to see him waving her over. She returns the gesture with a wave and a smile before heading over toward his table. After squeezing between two tables, she finally takes the seat across from him. The Professor nonchalantly checks his watch to see that it is 4:46. She is right on time. He looks up quickly at her and smiles.

"Hello, my dear."

"Hi Professor. So, what's this big assignment about?"

"Anne, I have been tasked with putting together a book. A group of investors contracted me and paid me quite well, might I add, to put a book together for them. A history book, so to speak."

"Really, wow that sounds like fun. What's it about," she asks excitedly.

The Professor sits up, straightening his back against the seat-back, and folds his newspaper in half.

"It's about a medieval tribe from Europe that I have been studying for some time. But the time has come where my supporters have informed me to pull all my notes together and write the damn book. I, however, am a man who loves the chase and the thrill of discovery. I can't stand writing it all down. It bores me to tears. So this is where you come in."

Anne's expression turns to puzzlement.

"Anne, I want *you* to write the book," he states.

"Me?"

"Yes, you my dear. I have been reading your papers long enough to know talent when I see it. All I need of you is to take dictation, expand on my notes, and tie everything into a historical timeline. Once it is finished, you will get credit with co-authoring the book."

He looks around, uncrosses his legs, and leans in a little closer to Anne. He speaks in a softer tone.

"Anne, you are my best student and extremely talented. You would do me proud to embark on this adventure with me."

Christina is standing in the doorway to the kitchen looking at the pair. Anne catches a quick glimpse of her moving her fist back and forth from her mouth while sticking her tongue against her cheek as if giving an imaginary blowjob. Rattled, Anne quickly focuses back on the Professor.

"Wow, Professor. I'm honored. It sounds like a lot of work though. What about my course load on top of all this? I think it might be too much for me right now."

"Not to worry, my dear. This semester is half way through, yes?"

"Yes," she responds.

"Right. Next semester you will take your final thesis course for your Masters."

Anne takes a long pause and questions his last statement.

"Wait. What? I'm not supposed to take that for two more semesters. Not till next January."

The Professor closes his eyes, looks down and calmly raises his hand, gesturing her to pause.

"Relax. I've already cleared it. Next semester you will take your final thesis course while working with me. Once the book is finished and published you will have amassed enough credits along with your paper to receive your Masters. All you have to do is say yes."

Anne's eyes widen as her jaw drops a bit. She stares at him in silence for a brief second in disbelief. She eventually snaps herself out of it and replies to him.

"Professor, this is an incredible opportunity. And thank you. Thank you very much. But, before I say yes, you know I have to talk to Rob about it. But, I'm sure he won't have a problem with it at all."

"Good. I'll expect an answer on Wednesday after class."

The Professor stands up, takes his overcoat, and places it over his arm.

"Good day to you, my dear and congratulations."

He slides by Anne who moves her legs aside to make room for him to pass. He gets halfway through the café then stops, turns and looks back to Anne. He gives her a smile and a nod. She gives him an awestruck smile in return as he turns and walks out into the early evening.

Anne sits for a few seconds watching the Professor leave.

Christina comes over and asks, "So what was that all about?"

Anne snaps out of her daze and awkwardly looks up at Christina. Christina hands her a cup of coffee, sits down beside her and asks again, "Well, what did he want?"

Anne turns and looks to her best friend, "You're never going to believe this."

The Professor is about four blocks from Durgin's when his walk home is suddenly disrupted. He is grabbed by the arm and pulled unceremoniously into the alleyway. Alarmed and momentarily confused, he is surprised to see that his assailants are the thugs from earlier in the day.

The leader, whose name is Krieger, pushes the Professor hard against the side of the building with his forearm up at the Professor's throat.

"Ow is the book coming, Professor? You sure seem to be takin' yo' fucking time. Are you 'aving fun with all this?"

His accent is clearly British but with a harsh street parlance.

Krieger's grip on the Professor's coat gets tighter as he slams him hard against the wall again.

The other two, Inns and Malachai, giggle and look around in nervous anticipation.

"Your contributors are getting anxious for its completion. Your time frame is comin' to an end Professor. Get it fucking done!" Krieger states in a guttural tone.

Just then, two upperclassmen walk by to see the Professor being assaulted by the trio.

"Hey," one of them yells. All three of them turn their heads. The two boys drop their books and run down the alley toward the encounter. One of the boys runs hard into Inns with his shoulder, knocking him down to the ground. He then faces Malachai and pushes him away.

The other student gets in Krieger's face and asks, "Is there a problem here, Professor?"

Inns gets up and gets chest to chest with the student that knocked him over.

"No problem," Krieger says "No problem at all."

He releases his grip on the Professor and straightens out the Professor's disheveled collar on his trench coat. He then slowly backs away with his arms up.

"We don't want any trouble 'er."

The three turn and retreat back down the alley but not before Krieger gives another smirk and a wink at the Professor.

"Those damn hooligans, and never an officer of the law around when you need one. Thank you boys for your assistance. If you'll excuse me, I'll be on my way now."

"You sure you're all right Professor," the student asks as he hands the Professor his newspaper.

"Yes, yes, quite all right boys. Off with you now, and thank you again."

The Professor hurriedly gathers himself and heads back down the sidewalk only at a slightly quicker pace.

# AN OPPORTUNITY

Rob had arrived home earlier than normal this evening from his graphic design studio that he owns downtown. Work has been very steady lately so he rewarded himself and his only employee, Pete, with closing the shop earlier than normal. His ulterior motive was so he could spend a little quality time with his new video game before Anne arrives home. Anne has never been a fan of Rob's video game habit. She feels that he gets too caught up in them, and that causes him to be grumpy and irritable. Rob, of course, vehemently denies such allegations but does feel it is a nice release from the pressures of running his small business.

Running his own business can be stressful at times but he never lets it get to him. The simple fact that owning his own business brings him a great amount of pride.

Throughout his life, Rob had always felt he had a touch of Charlie Brown luck, a feeling that the whole world was against him, or forever being behind the eight ball. When he was 15, his dad died of lung cancer. Of course, he smoked his entire life but he was a hard worker and was very influential in Rob developing a strong work ethic.

His mom died just two years later from a heart attack and he was left with his older brother Tom, who raised him.

After a few dates Anne had revealed to Rob that her parents had died in a car crash when she was 13. They both shared to one another that they each needed therapy afterwards to help cope with the ensuing feelings. This connection helped them form a strong bond to one another. Both share similar family values and someday wish to have a large family.

Rob had tried many things growing up but never really excelled at anything. He did make it to college on his own but was denied financial aid. He wound up paying for school with student loans but struggled scholastically throughout. Anne was paramount in helping Rob get through college. Without her aid and support, he never would have graduated. Eventually, he graduated with a degree in graphic design. Now he finds himself here, thankful for two things in his life, his business, and meeting his best friend and the love of his life, Anne.

She always found school to be easy and excelled. As a result, her college was paid for primarily by scholarships. That has always caused a bit of jealousy with him that he never shares with her. His Charlie Brown luck compared to the way everything falls into place for her. For all she has done for him, being that one person in his eyes that believed in and supported him, he knows how lucky he is to have her in his life. That is enough for him to keep those sentiments bottled up.

For now, though, Rob is content to melt into his favorite couch, push all his stress to the back of his mind and zone out to his game. Sometimes he'll play for hours before he realizes the time. It is a bit of contention for Anne but she tolerates it because deep down she knows it makes him happy. She knows he works hard and puts in many hours to support her goal of getting her Master's degree. She can overlook his habit.

After her meeting with the Professor, Anne hung out with Christina for a bit and then hurries home to tell Rob the news about the proposal. Within a few minutes of leaving Durgin's, she arrives at her home, which is just off Main Street, and a short walk from the center of town. The dwelling is actually half of a duplex that she and Rob chose because of its proximity to the school and to Rob's graphic design business downtown.

Whenever she walks up onto the porch, she is reminded of when her parents, who were deeply religious, used to tell her that couples shouldn't live together unless they are at least engaged. After Rob found this place, Anne informed him of their wishes. Not missing a beat, he went out the next day, got her the ring of her dreams, and proposed to her on this porch. After all this time, she can't believe their story together and how lucky she is to be with him.

While fumbling for her keys in her purse, she gets slightly annoyed that her ring keeps catching on everything. She shakes her purse a final time to locate the jingle of her keys. She retrieves the keys and throws her purse over her shoulder. Unlocking the door, she rushes in, dropping her bags beside the door. The duplex is small and now with the shorter fall days, very dark.

"Rob?" she calls as she flicks the light on in the hallway.

A moment later he responds.

"In the living room."

She peeks down the hallway where she sees a dim light coming from the living room at the end of the hall. Enthusiastically, she skips in to tell her fiancé about the Professor's proposal.

Upon entering the living room, she finds Rob slumped on the couch playing his game. His eyes are fixated on the TV, the only movements he makes are the swift flicking of his fingers on the game controller. She walks around the couch and sits on his lap, purposely blocking his view.

"Hey, hey, I'm playing here," he protests.

"Honey, pause the game just for a second."

"Ok, ok, hold on." He leans to the side, peering around Anne, staring at the screen and fumbling for the button to pause the game. He presses a few buttons on his controller. Now with the game on hold, he slumps back into the couch and stares at her.

"What's up," he asks a little perturbed.

"You're not going to believe this. You know Professor Caerwyn, right?"

"Of course I do, why?"

"Well, Professor Caerwyn has asked me to write a book with him."

"A book? Wow, that's pretty cool. How did all this come about?"

"I have no idea, he just called me to his desk after class and asked me to meet him at Durgin's. When I got there, he asked me to help him with this book he's working on."

"Interesting. So how's that gonna work?"

"Well, listen to this. This is what he's proposed. When this fall semester gets over, he wants me to start working with him."

"Hold on," Rob interrupts "How are you going to fit that into your schedule? You're going to have a full line up of classes next semester. And what about skiing during the break? We've already planned our trip."

"Well, if you would slow down and give me second to explain."

"Alright, alright. Go ahead."

She pauses for a moment, glaring at him to make sure he won't interrupt again.

"I'm listening," he says impatiently.

"First off, the ski trip is not in jeopardy, Ok? Now, as I was saying, at the end of this semester I will start working with the Professor. His plans are to hopefully finish up by the end of next semester. Now, instead of taking the classes I'm already signed up for, I will take my final thesis course instead. At the end of this school year, I'll be done with that course and finished with the book. Now get this. The Professor and the school will grant me all the credits I need to get my Masters and graduate early."

"Are you serious? Even though you are supposed to be three semesters away from finishing up?"

"Yeah, but by helping the Professor write his book, he said the school will grant me enough credits to allow me to skip all those courses. It's an unbelievable opportunity and I'll be published right out of college."

"Wow. I don't know what to say except that's awesome. Now I know why you're so excited. But, before we decide, how much time is this going to take? I mean writing a book, isn't that supposed to take years? It sounds a little too good to be true to me."

Anne gets up off the couch, quickly collecting her thoughts. She knows Rob all too well and was expecting a lot of skepticism from him. She walks around the coffee table, turning slightly away from him as she speaks.

"The Professor has already done all the leg work. He has all the notes, research-everything. That info just needs to be pulled together and written. I would be surprised if it took any longer than four to five months."

"Four to five months! Aw man, that's gonna suck! You're going to be so busy. When am I ever going to see you," he bemoans.

Anne turns back towards him. She walks back to the couch and slides down beside him while draping her arm around his shoulders.

"Come on Rob, I'm already locked into almost two more years of school doing it my way. Don't forget we're paying for those two years. Going this way, it'll only be one more semester. Why can't you see the benefit of this for us?"

Rob pauses before speaking. He does realize how important this is to Anne. He also understands the financial savings this could mean to the struggling couple. He looks up at Anne, her facial expression pleading for his approval.

The best he can do is smirk at her. She cocks her head, perplexed by the expression and smiles in hopeful anticipation.

"Yeah, I guess that makes sense. I just don't want anything to interfere with, you know, *our* plans," he says as he caresses the side of Anne's face.

"Ever since we talked, I've just been so anxious to start our family."

Anne leans into Rob and hugs him gently while she lays her head on his broad shoulders. He reciprocates the gesture. She caresses the hair on the back of his head and begins to speak in a softer reassuring tone.

"I know. And I know our plans are important to you and you know they're important to me. But, this book could be very helpful for me and us. Again, if we go our way it'll take two years, with us paying through the nose. If we take this opportunity, it'll be just one semester with virtually no cost to us. That means that we can start our plans together sooner."

Sliding her leg over Rob's lap, she positions herself on top of him again.

He gets quiet as he sees the excitement in Anne's face dwindle. He does, however, understand that this is the right thing for Anne and ultimately does give in to her request.

"Well, I guess when you put it that way, you're right. Doing the book is the better way to go."

Rob pauses. Anne is now all smiles.

"Go ahead and write your book. But the Professor better not think he's getting you all to himself. He needs to know that you've got a man at home who'll be needing some attention."

He leans back into the couch placing his hands behind his head.

He looks at her with puppy eyes making the goofiest romantic expression he can. Anne laughs and leans into him.

"Don't you worry, man, you'll get all the attention you need."

She hugs him again and pulls back to look at him.

"Thank you, honey. You have no idea what this means to me."

Anne squeezes hard again and finishes the embrace with a kiss.

# NIGHTTIME FUN

A quarter passed midnight, just outside of town, Krieger, Malachai, and Inns have gathered underneath an overpass. During the day, this is a popular bike path for joggers and bikers, but at night, it is silent and desolate. The tunnel leading under the road is fairly wide, allowing for bicyclists to pass by one another with ease. It is dimly lit at each end by two small lights that are covered by a steel mesh, preventing any would-be vandals from breaking them.

In the tunnel, the three have stumbled upon a hitchhiker, asleep in a sleeping bag for the night. This will be a treat for them to torment the weary traveler. Inns picks up the hiker's backpack and drops it on his head.

"Aaahh," the hiker bemoans. "What the hell?"

Malachai and Inns get excited about their prey. Malachai picks up the backpack and dumps the young man's belongings all over the ground.

"Hey, what is your problem," the hitchhiker stands up and protests.

His outcries only annoy the two.

"Shut up," replies Inns as Malachai pushes the young man down into a puddle.

He gets up and implores his assailants to stop.

"Come on guys, give me a break. Just give me my stuff and I'll get out of here."

Malachai who had been exploring the man's belongings replies, "You're not going anywhere until we decide."

He tosses the backpack into the puddle in disgust.

"Hey! Come on, man. Those are my only dry clothes," he yells.

Malachai rushes over to the hitchhiker and pushes him hard up against the wall. The young traveler turns his head and pulls his hands up to protect his face but as he does this, Malachai delivers a fierce blow to his stomach. He doubles over in pain clutching his gut and coughing in agony. Eventually the embattled traveler collapses to the ground into the fetal position. He struggles to speak as the pain in his gut worsens.

"Please guys, I don't want any trouble. What do you want? I have a little cash I can give you, just let me go," he pleads.

Inns, who is getting aggravated by this petty display of begging, walks over and kicks the traveler hard in the ribs. The force of the blow knocks the wind out of the hitchhiker who gasps for air.

"Stop whining, you little bitch," Inns demands.

Malachai finds the statement humorous and giggles to himself.

Lying on the wet ground and desperate for help, the hitchhiker screams out.

"Help! Help me! Somebody, please!"

Angered by the boy's continued defiance, Malachai runs over and yells.

"He told you to shut up!"

Malachai kicks violently at the young man. His big heavy boots delivering powerful, bruising blows. Inns joins in the attack and the hiker's screams start to wane.

Krieger clearly isn't as enthused with the entertainment his cohorts are partaking in. He walks away from the scene over to the base of the steep embankment leading up to the road. The hill itself is blanketed in thick grass and shrubs. It's a chilly evening and as he stares up the hill to the sky, he amuses himself watching the vapor of his breath dissipate into the night air. A car passes by on the road overhead disrupting the scene, only momentarily. He glances at his friends who have cupped their hands over the hiker's mouth while the car speeds away into the distance.

Krieger looks back at the sky. His expression indicates impatience, as if he is waiting for something. Seconds later, that something occurs when the sound of his cell phone rings from within his worn out leather jacket. He reaches for the phone, flips it open and raises it to his ear.

"Ello," he mumbles.

The sound on the other end is the unmistakable sound of Beauregard's voice.

"Have you been watching the Professor like I asked?"

"Yeah, we *talked* to him the other day and told him to quit fucking around and finish the book. I think he got the message."

"Good, the sooner he finishes the book the better. We are nearly finished planning our operation. But first, the book must be completed. The truce will end when the book is done."

"Ya know B, I don't understand why all the loyalty? Why don't we just put the plan into action and forget about this horseshit truce?"

"Krieger, there are many pack leaders out there who feel that it is of critical importance for the survival of our race that this book be written. You more than anyone should know that in this day and age, if you don't have your word, then you have nothing to bargain with. We will hold with the truce, am I understood?"

"Yeah, I s'pose," replies a reluctant Krieger.

"Remember, once the book is done, then we can initiate our plans."

"B, I know the story. I don't need a fuckin' re-cap, especially from you. And I hope I don't need to remind you of our bargain. You better not fuck with us. My people have never been a fan of yours and if you deceive us in any way, I swear, you won't be around long."

"Your people are not fans of mine? Well, are they fans of the King and his loathsome kingdom?"

"No," Krieger mumbles.

"Then mind your place and hold true to your alliance," Beauregard snaps.

"When this is over, both our clans will be much wealthier as well as rulers of a new Kingdom."

"Yeah, right, whatever, anyways I gotta run. Me and the boys are getting ready to eat."

"Keep on the Professor and make sure he is working on the book. He is the only thing preventing us from moving forward. Enjoy your meal. I'll be in touch. Ciao."

"Whatever." Krieger snaps the phone shut as he drops it back in his pocket. He looks back up at the night sky still amusing himself with his breath in the night air.

Just behind him, a huge beast slowly peers over Krieger's shoulder. The beast lets out a low-pitched growl as fresh blood is dripping from its mouth. A startled Krieger turns to look up at the monster. Before him, towering above, stands a lycan. Not man, and not wolf, but a combination of the two. The giant head, clearly resembling that of a wolf with tall ears and a protruding snout, looms ferociously over Krieger. The body has more human attributes to it with a broad muscular chest and thick arms. It boasts huge hands, each with five digits but it is the razor sharp claws on the end of each finger that are indeed a menacing sight. The creature is covered entirely in a thick, dark, matted fur. Its legs look more like a wolf standing on its haunches however the creature is still able to stand upright with ease.

"Inns, I hope you two left me some," Krieger states.

The beast nods his head in the affirmative. Krieger pushes the lycan aside and walks towards what's left of the hitchhiker. Another lycan is kneeling down, hunched over the body. Malachai, who has also transformed into a lycan, is frantically gorging himself on the bloodied flesh. Krieger runs over and kicks the beast in the mid-section knocking him a few feet away onto the ground. The beast quickly recovers, jumping to his feet while simultaneously letting out an angry roar directed at Krieger.

Krieger continues to stalk him, getting right in the lycan's face. Krieger points his finger almost into its eye and shouts, "Ow many times do I have to tell you, Mal, you have to leave me some, too."

Malachai turns his massive head to the side in disgust. Krieger turns to walk back to the bloodied corpse. He drops down to his knees, hunkering over the body. He stares at the remains for a second then looks up at the underside of the bridge. He closes his eyes and begins to change.

# COLLABORATION

The sun is just about to set on a disagreeably cold December day. The late afternoon darkness is frustrating to many New Englanders but is part of the charisma that makes living there so unique. The region has already seen its share of early snowfall, and a mound of fresh snow borders the sidewalk on which Anne walks.

She arrives at the Professor's front walk precisely at 5pm. The walkway leading up to his house has been meticulously free of any snow or ice. Anne checks her watch again to ensure she isn't late. The two had made the decision to get a head start on their endeavor by beginning the project during the Christmas break, much to Rob's dismay. She figured she had plenty of spare time during the break, as her only responsibilities were some part-time hours at Durgin's that were promised to her as favor from the owner.

The wide, granite walk leading to the house made her realize the magnitude of the Professor's success. His house is anything but modest. It is a massive three-story Victorian with a deep farmer's porch, which encompasses the entire front of the house and wraps down the left side around to the back.

The large granite steps feel hard under Anne's feet as she bounces up them. She half expects the wooden planks of the deck to squeak under her footsteps but to her surprise they'll feel as solid as the native granite. She knocks on the thick wooden door hoping it was loud enough to be heard inside. A moment passes and that concern is put to rest when the Professor swings open the door.

"Ah, Anne. Come in, come in."

"Thank you, Professor. I can't believe how freezing it is today."

"Yes, it is," he pauses pondering her grammatically incorrect statement. "Good thing I have a fire going that you can warm yourself by. Follow me if you will."

Anne enters the house and the Professor closes the door behind her. She pauses for him, then falls in line behind the Professor as they both walk down the main hallway.

She marvels at the innate woodwork all around the house. It all appears to be left to its natural color with only a few glossy layers of lacquer giving a hint to the craftsmanship invested in this grand manor. Everywhere she looks is wood, decorated with trim and ornate hand carved inlays.

The Professor peers over his shoulder and interrupts her curiosity.

"Are you ready to start the adventure?"

"Yes Professor, I'm very anxious to get started. There is one problem though."

The Professor stops in his tracks, turns and looks at her with an anxious expression.

"Oh. And what's that?"

"Well, for starters," she says with a grin, "I'm still not entirely sure what the book is about yet."

"Oh, my goodness, forgive my vagueness. Well, we're here. Come into the study where we'll be working and I'll fill you in."

The scholar has led Anne almost to the end of the hall where he has stopped by two large sliding doors on his left. He opens one of the doors revealing a large, dimly lit antique study. There are books floor to ceiling on both sides of the room with two black iron ladders that slide on a track across each wall. In front of them is an immense stone fireplace and true to his word, there is a fire going warming the room. Anne was fixated on its size and guessed the mantle must sit about six feet high. On both sides of the fireplace, mounted high on the wall, are two stuffed animal heads; one a huge boars head and the other an elk head with large sprawling antlers.

In the middle of the room sit two brown leather couches facing each other on each side of the fireplace. There are also two long, antique tables on the left side of the room. On one of them, Anne could see dozens of old books. The books are stacked four and five high and most of them seem to be very old. On the other table are what appear to be a dozen or so old scrolls laid out across it. Some of the scrolls are rolled up while others are lying flat, as if they had recently been examined.

On the opposite side of the room from the tables sits an oversized antique desk with a large flat screen monitor and a computer beside it.

"This is it my dear. I have amassed every piece of information I could find and it is all located there."

The Professor points to the two tables.

"Your work station is over there," he points to the desk. "That is where our masterpiece will be written."

"Professor," sighs Anne with a smirk.

"Yes, what is it?"

"What," she pauses to be dramatic, "is the book about?"

"Ah, yes, well, why don't you have a seat and we'll get started." He gestures her toward one of the couches as he takes Anne's coat and hangs it on a stand by the door. She drops her bag by the computer desk and walks over to the couch where she takes a seat. Expecting to sink into the nice plush cushions, she is caught off guard by how firm the couch actually is.

The professor retreats behind the opposite couch and places both hands on the back of it. He looks at Anne and begins.

"The book is about a hidden civilization, if you will, that existed in Europe about 450 to 500 years ago. This Kingdom, as I like to call it, was very powerful and wealthy. What made it significant is that the people involved in it worshipped wolves."

"Wolves? Really? That's rather unique. I can't say I've ever heard of anything like that before. Except for," she takes a pause while pondering her thoughts, "well maybe the appreciation that Native Americans had for them."

"Quite right, my dear. As a matter of fact, the only real documentation of a culture similar is of some Turkic and Mongolian peoples who worshipped them in ancient China. They were however, very few in number. That is what makes this Kingdom so fascinating."

"Now, before we go any further with this Anne, I must demand your complete and utter secrecy about this project. No one can know the subject matter on which we're writing, at least until it's done. I cannot stress enough how imperative it is that you agree to this or we can go no further."

"I guess but what's the big deal? Isn't this just a simple research project," she asks.

"Anne, let's just say that my—excuse me, our employers demand its secrecy, at least for the time being. With the huge collection of data done so far, I'm afraid I must insist."

"Alright, of course, Professor. Whatever you ask. It's your project and if those are the rules, then those are the rules."

"Splendid, thank you my dear. I knew I could count on you to be trustworthy."

She stands and walks over to the table as the Professor inquisitively watches her expression. Her eyes scan over the table as her hands wade through the vast collection of ancient books, texts, and artifacts.

"Where did you get all these?"

"Most are borrowed from private collectors who don't know what they are. Some, I have actually recovered and others, believe it or not, are from some of the descendants of the Kingdom. To answer your next question, yes, they are the primary backers of this project. They have asked me to research and write the book so they can have their spot in history validated."

"Wow, Professor, this is incredible."

"That is why I chose you, Anne, for your passion and intellect. I knew you'd be excited."

Anne makes her way over to the computer and sits.

"So, let's get started. What were you thinking of calling it?"

"Well, to be honest I quite fancied the title, The Kingdom."

"Then The Kingdom it is."

At the top of the computer screen, a flashing cursor awaits her. She types, the name appearing in bold letters across the top of the monitor. She looks up at the Professor.

"Alright, let's go. Start talking."

The Professor looks over at her smiling face and smiles himself. He closes his eyes, takes a deep breath, and looks toward the ceiling. His head slowly falls and he opens his eyes.

He clears his throat and begins.

"My dear, let me start by telling you a bedtime story. It isn't a happy one but one in which the followers believe was the beginning of their legacy. It begins like this."

"An old hermit woman, whom some believe to be a witch, lived in the deep woods of old Bavaria in Europe. She lived by herself for many years and her only companion was a pet.

A very unique pet, a wolf."

"One day, a farmer and his wife took residence at the edge of the forest to start their own farm. Year after year, the farmer grew his fields bigger and bigger, to a point where his land started to abut the old woman's tiny parcel. As well, the farmer began to feel more and more uneasy about the witch and her uncharacteristic practices. He asks her many times if she would consider leaving, but she refuses. One day while hunting in the woods, he sees the witch's wolf running through the thicket. The farmer, still annoyed by her defiance, decides to send a message to the old woman."

"Taking aim at the beast with his bow, he sends an arrow deep into the animal's chest, killing it instantly. He drags the carcass to the old woman's house where he finds her harvesting some herbs in her garden. He throws the wolf down in front of her and claims that if she doesn't move away, her fate will be the same as her pet. He presumes his actions will scare her enough to finally leave."

"So distraught over her pet's demise, the witch devises a plan to exact revenge on her new neighbors. Before burying the wolf, she cuts a fresh wound and drains some of its blood. She mixes the blood with some other ingredients and creates a mysterious brew. With help from one of her many spiritual books, she places a powerful curse on the concoction."

"Later that week, under the light of a bright, full moon, she makes the short journey through the woods to her neighbor's farm. Sneaking into the farmer's house, she silently creeps up the stairs into the couple's bedroom. Dark shadows conceal her every move as she makes her way over to the farmer's wife's side of the bed. She is many months pregnant and sleeping quite soundly. The witch carefully pulls off the bed covers exposing the young woman's pregnant body.

She quietly opens the satchel containing the potion and slowly pours the blood onto the wife's pregnant abdomen."

"The story goes that the wolf's blood instantly absorbed into her skin like water in beach sand. The wife abruptly awakens and leaps out of the bed screaming and clutching at her abdomen. The sensation feels as if her body were on fire and her agonizing screams confirm her pain. The alarmed farmer stumbles out of bed. His concern for his wife is turned to rage when he sees the old witch laughing in the corner of the room. Confused and fearful, he takes the small chair sitting beside the bed and strikes down on her with all his might. He continues his attack, beating the old woman until he is certain there is no life left in her. He immediately checks on his wife. Consoling her until the pain eventually subsides."

"So, as the story goes, life goes on, or so the farmer thinks. Months later, the wife eventually gives birth to a son. The birth is horrific and she nearly loses her life in the process. She does survive but later on, after years of trying, the couple finds that she doesn't have the ability to bare any more children. To make matters worse, they soon discover that their only son is to become the first ever werewolf."

Anne's eyebrows suddenly raise and she stops typing.

"Werewolf? Wait a minute, Professor, you said they worshipped wolves. This is beginning to sound a little bit fairy tale-ish."

"Now don't get ahead of yourself Anne, what I said was true, my dear. They did not believe they were werewolves but they did believe their founding King was a lycanthrope, one that has the ability to change into wolf form. Remember, I said this was a story, not fact."

"Fair enough. Go on Professor."

"OK then. Time passes for the farmer and his small family. Everything about that fateful night was all but forgotten until the boy reaches adolescence. He becomes increasingly wild with uncontrollable urges. He strikes out at his parents and spends most of his time in the woods hunting small animals. This is when the instinct to *feed* begins to take control of him. Then, one night as a full moon shone, an animalistic rage consumes the boy. No longer human, and just an animal at heart, the boy goes wild and kills both of his parents, tearing their bodies apart with his bare hands. Their blood curbs the boy's kill instinct and he soon returns to his human state of mind."

"As he grows older, he comes to grips with certain aspects of his curse. Over time he gets a better understanding of how to control the rage. He also learns that consuming human flesh is the only way to satiate it."

"Unwittingly, while fighting with one of his friends, he bites him. He later learns that by doing so, his friend became what he is. From that point on, his loneliness drives him to create more like him. He sets out to infect others and create a tribe of creatures like himself. First, it is his lovers, then people close to him, and eventually warriors. That, my dear, is how the Kingdom begins."

"You weren't kidding. There isn't a happy ending there. You said though that he infected others. His followers couldn't turn into monsters?" Anne asks.

"No, not as far as I can tell. During their rituals, they would don the hides of wolves that they had killed. By doing so, that would represent the transformation to beast. It's just a ritual my dear. Sometimes you need to have a little faith in stories."

"True. Look at Jesus," she retorts.

"Exactly my point, and I think on that note, I'm beginning to feel a bit tired, so let's call it a night, shall we?"

"We shall," Anne says with a giggle.

"How about we continue tomorrow. Say, around seven?"

"Works for me, what time is it anyway?" looking at her watch. "Oh, it's only 9:15. It's not too late. Rob will be happy to see me home early on our first night."

"Rob is a very fortunate young man."

"Yeah, well don't tell him that. He's convinced he's the real life Charlie Brown."

Anne gathers her things and pulls on her coat that was hanging near the door. She squeezes her bag between her legs as she finishes buttoning up her coat.

"Ok, Professor, I'll see you tomorrow."

"I can't wait, you be safe out there."

"I will, and thanks again Professor for such a great opportunity."

"My dear, thank you," he replies.

Anne heads out the door and spots some ice on the sidewalk. She skips ahead and slides the entire length of the patch. The Professor stands in the doorway and watches with a calm smile until she is out of sight. He shakes his head and slowly moves back into his house. A snowball hits the front door and explodes beside his head. Some frozen bits land on the Professor's face.

Surprised, the Professor turns to see Krieger, Malachai, and Inns standing by his walk. Krieger just stands there staring down the Professor with his arms crossed and a deadpan look on his face. The other two are giggling at one another and tossing snowballs in the air.

The Professor's disposition turns from pleasant to furious as he does his best to stare down Krieger. He slowly backs in through his doorway and slams the door. The front lights all go out as Krieger turns and walks away. The other two follow.

# HISTORY

The following night, the Professor expands on the basic history of the Kingdom. What he had previously told Anne she found unbelievable but what he will explain to her tonight will be unfathomable.

Walking around the study, the Professor recites from memory while Anne feverishly types away on the computer. She is so efficient that the Professor never has to slow down for her to catch up. His memory is his only hindrance. Even when he rambles on, she never falls behind. She has taken enough classes with the Professor to understand his way of thinking and what specific points to extract from what he is saying.

She, on the other hand, is amazed at how much the Professor can just churn out without so much as looking at a single note. This is one of the qualities she has long admired about him as a teacher.

"Ok, my dear, are you ready for a history lesson?"

"Yes sir," she says coyly.

"Ok, let's begin with a chapter entitled The Basic Principles of the Kingdom. In its infancy, some five hundred years ago, the Werewolf Kingdom had only several hundred wolves or members scattered around Europe, and obviously at that point, no one had made the trek across the Atlantic Ocean."

"Excuse me Professor. I gotta tell ya, this whole werewolf thing is kinda weird. Isn't there another term we can refer to them as? I mean, you yourself said that they are people only pretending to be wolves. They are not transforming into wolves, like we see on TV. If they are wearing the hides of wolves and all, then by definition they're not really werewolves. They're humans, right?"

For the first time since they started the project together, the Professor squints his eyes and looks at Anne rather sharply. Reacting to his stern gaze, she leans back into her chair sinking below her computer screen.

There is a long silence before the Professor speaks and when he does, his tone indicates he is a slight bit irritated.

"Quite right, my dear," in a combative tone, "let's be technical and call a spade a spade."

He pauses again holding his chin and looking up at the ceiling. He refocuses his glare back to Anne to survey her reaction to his tone which, as yet, she has none. She just stares at him while feeling suddenly very awkward.

"Well, my dear, if you feel werewolf is an inappropriate term, then let us work through a word that you may feel is more appropriate. We could start with the word lycanthrope derived from the Greek word *lukanthropos*. As you well know, that breaks down to two words, *lukos* meaning wolf and *anthropos* meaning man or human. That will eventually evolve into the English term lycanthropes which is a person or persons who believes themselves to be a wolf."

The Professor rants on in an irritated tone and refuses to observe Anne's uncomfortableness to his mild outburst. He continues.

"No, I still think that's a bit much. How about if we shorten it shall we? Yes, shortened, of course."

"How about we use the increasingly popular word lycan, which is one suffering from the lycanthropy. The problem we face here is the two beliefs about lycanthropy. The first is that lycans themselves believe they have the magical ability to assume the form and characteristics of a wolf. The second is a medical term for which psychologists believe that lycanthropy is a mental illness for which people demonstrate qualities of wolves and believe that they are indeed wolves."

"It is a popular term though, one which many people do recognize. Maybe, that word will be the best. How about that? Will the word lycan be adequate for you, my dear?"

Rather surprised at the Professor's sudden change in demeanor she remains sunken down behind her monitor. Her face is flushed as she quietly utters, "Yes sir, that sounds fine."

"Good," the Professor replies sternly. He turns away from Anne to gather his thoughts and recall where he last left off.

"Now, in the Kingdom, there is a hierarchy that is led by a King. Kings are commonly young and strong with a group of elders whom he will often rely on for advice during his rule. In order to keep the Kingdom strong and thriving, the Wolf King should have at least one heir to the throne. If he fails to do so, he will undoubtedly risk attacks to his reign or upon his demise, the elders will choose a new worthy king to replace him."

"Not encompassed within the Kingdom's realm, there exist other clans or packs. Some of them are small while others are quite large. These clans live outside the Kingdom's domain and protection and often do, well, pretty much whatever they want. They have been known to be careless and reckless around humans and because of this, many of these clans had been hunted almost to extinction."

"These clans are rival to the Kingdom and are rough and very often destitute. They were commonly uneducated and nomadic. They'd move from one area to the next, killing and stealing until they were forced to move on."

"Most of them despise everything the Kingdom represents yet they crave its wealth and power. Every now and again they drum up alliances with one another to wage war for the throne. To date, no rogue clan has ever successfully captured the throne."

"Professor, if I may?" Anne interrupts.

"Of course child," he replies with his usual calm demeanor.

"Was there, well, is there an actual castle where all this took place?"

The Professor lightly chuckles and states, "It would seem that way but not quite. Let me explain. In the area we know as the Austrian Alps, there was a mountainous region where there was a sort of stronghold, where the Kingdom existed for many years. It was a system of caves and walls that were easily defendable that I suppose, could be considered a castle, so to speak. For many years this was where the Kingdom existed. Members would eventually settle in the outlying region and farm the land or take up businesses. They would take what they needed and contribute the rest to the Kingdom with the understanding that if they ever needed anything, support would be granted."

"So, what you're saying is," Anne interrupts, "if any Kingdom member ran into any trouble or came under attack, then the other members would come to their aid? And who would attack them, for example?"

"Oh, it could be anything from thieves or other farmers, to those rival clans we spoke about," he replies.

"So, these other clans, why wouldn't they want to be part of the Kingdom and why couldn't they just join up?"

"That's a good question, Anne, which leads us to what makes the Kingdom so unique. There is one major difference between the rogue clans and the Kingdom and that difference is how they gain entry or membership into the organization. Rogue clans, because they have no hierarchy, commonly have a lot of discord among their people. They lose members to infighting, runaways, or possibly from being hunted. They think nothing of killing their own in a dispute and when the clan starts to diminish in size, they just find an unsuspecting human and force them to join. Sometimes they might try to bribe rival clan members to join with them. It's a sort of power in numbers thing."

The Professor stops talking and walks over to the table opposite Anne's desk. He surveys the pile of artifacts, specifically looking for something. His eyes finally key in on a small, tattered leather book. He frees the book from under a mountain of larger books and flips halfway through to a certain section. Once he finds the info he needs, he continues to lecture again while leafing through the pages.

"Typically a new member is an outsider or human. On very rare occasions they might allow a person from a rival clan to join but that is very uncommon. To join into the Kingdom, new members must be presented during a special ceremony called by the elders. First, you must be sponsored by a Kingdom member. To be sponsored means the member sees characteristics in you that are worthy of membership."

"Characteristics like what?" Anne asks.

"Well, they could be wealth, business acrimony, trade skills, or maybe excellent leadership abilities. Once you are invited to this meeting, you will be judged by the circle of elders. From that point you will either be selected to join or not. If you are not selected, then you are executed."

Anne's head lifts up abruptly from behind her monitor.

"Excuse me? Did you say executed?"

"Yes, my dear, executed."

"That sounds extreme."

"Think for a moment, Anne. This Kingdom has hidden its wealth and members from society for hundreds of years. The reason for this is simple, secrecy means security. Thus the secrecy, even now my dear. Imagine if modern day society learned of this organizations existence and how it would be perceived in today's world. They would be persecuted for their beliefs and questioned about their wealth. Secrecy is the key."

"If you fail to pass the Circle of Elders then you are not part of the Kingdom. Now you are aware of the Kingdom's existence and are considered a threat. For the Kingdom to survive, that threat must be destroyed. So the wolf, pardon me, lycan member must be absolutely sure of whom he is sponsoring for membership and that they can pass the test. And the test is not the same for every new member."

"Professor, that is simply incredible. To think an organization could be so invested in itself and its development through the people it recruits is amazing. Also, the fact that it was that long ago is unreal. They were generations ahead of their time with thinking like that."

Anne falls back against her seat. The Professor turns to her, knowing from her expression she is now starting to connect the dots.

"Professor, if they were following those practices then, and we're putting this book together now for current members and descendants—"

"Yes, go on," he responds eagerly.

"Then these people must have a lot of money. A lot of old money, so to speak."

The Professor grins. His emotions are like that of a proud father with his child. He expects this kind of collaboration with her and is one of the many reasons he chose her. He loves teaching someone who is eager to learn. He proudly responds to her question.

"Anne, these people are among the wealthiest, most powerful, and influential people in the world."

She leans forward and rests her elbows on the desk with her hands together as if she were praying.

"And yet," she interrupts, "their only peculiarity is that they think they're wolves. I find that fascinating. How influential these people are but they are completely unaware that they are delusional."

The Professor rolls his eyes.

Anne slumps back in her chair staring at the wall trying to wrap her head around the sudden realization of just how prestigious this book could be. The Professor, realizing Anne's awe, refocuses her back to the present.

"Anne, if we could continue, please?"

She snaps her attention back to him.

"Oh yeah, sure."

Leaning forward and scanning over her notes, Anne resumes with her questioning.

"Now, Professor. Could you expand on those special entry meetings, the elder thingy?"

"Of course. The Circle of Elders, my dear."

The Professor pauses while he looks down at his watch. It reads 7:59. The chime from the old long-case clock by the wall confirms that it is now 8 pm. He begins to describe the ceremony for admission into the Kingdom.

# MEMBERSHIP

Thousands of miles across the Atlantic, hidden deep in the region of Bavaria, it is 2 am. Fifteen of the Kingdom's elders convene in a large stone chamber.

This room is hidden inside an old sanctuary owned by the Kingdom. Its shape resembles a half moon with a tall stonewall making up the arc portion of the half circle. There is also a wooden wall connecting the two ends of the arc that boasts a set of massive, wooden double doors. These doors are the only entrance into the arena.

Atop the stone wall, there are fifteen alcoves in which each elders are seated during the ceremony. They are located high above the floor, which is thick with sand.

Torches, hung high up on the walls, are evenly spaced to provide light. Large candles sit on the wall behind the elders illuminating their seats of prestige. High above in the middle the ceiling, there is an oculus that is open to night air. Tonight, the sky is clear and star-studded.

The elders are dressed in their ceremonial blue robes with the crest of the Kingdom embroidered on their chests. The talk is silenced as one of the elders claps his hands twice indicating the start of the membership ritual. The doors to the room open and a member of the Kingdom enters. Behind him is a new potential that he has recommended. The newcomer is known as a potential until he is granted the rite of member.

The elder, seated in the center, raises his hand gesturing the men to come forward. They walk to the center of the room, one followed by the other. The member starts to speak of the newcomer's talents and personality and why he should be allowed to join the Kingdom. The potential looks around in awe. He is astounded at the architecture but also anxious about the possibilities of joining the Kingdom.

"Circle of Elders, I bring forth a potential. I have known this man for many years. In that time, he has shown a dedication to advance himself, his friends, and a strong business sense that I feel will help grow the Kingdom in its endeavors in the future. His dedication is strong and I feel confident recommending him for membership."

A few brief moments pass and the elders stare in silence at the potential. They sense his nervousness and lean over to one another whispering and passing notes back and forth. This goes on for some minutes. The two men down on the floor can hear nothing of what is being said.

One of the elders off to the left abruptly stands up and leaps from his seat into the arena. In mid-air, he transforms into a lycan. He lands with tremendous force a few feet in front of the potential. Terrified, the young man screams and stumbles backwards to the ground. The huge lycan elder towers over the potential, peering at the nervous man. The potential turns his head in fear as the lycan sniffs about his head and chest.

The beast rears back while maintaining a wary eye on him. He stands up tall on his haunches and speaks to the potential. His voice is deep, throaty, and menacing.

"Becoming one of us will not cure you of your cowardice. Dedication does not make up for lack of bravery."

The lycan leans over the man once again sniffing the potential with his enormous snout.

"I smell too much fear in you."

Without hesitation, the lycan swiftly slashes down upon the potential with his claw. The powerful strike lands on the man's head, crushing his skull, killing him instantly.

The central seated elder motions the member to leave with a flick of his hand.

The disappointed Kingdom member nods his head in acknowledgement, turns, and exits back out the wooden doors. They close behind him with a solid thud.

The lycan still on the floor of the room stands up and looks to the central elder, who motions for him to stay where he is. The doors to the room open again and another Kingdom member leads in a new potential. The lycan turns, sizing up the new entrant while stepping aside, allowing them room to move past.

This potential does not seem alarmed at all by what he sees in the room. He reaches the center of the room, confidently standing beside his sponsor just in front of the corpse on the floor.

He is introduced to the room.

"Circle of Elders, I bring forth a potential," the member begins.

But before he can continue, the central elder raises his hand for silence. The lycan walks over to the potential and takes position behind him. The potential does not seem phased by the proximity of the enormous creature to himself. He maintains his focus on the other elders above him as they commence to engage in debate amongst themselves. The conversations are generally quiet but some quickly get heated as hands get raised in the air as debates rage on. After a few minutes and surprisingly not a single question being asked to the potential, the elders all finally nod their heads in agreement. The head elder stands and speaks.

"We find you worthy of membership to the Kingdom and grant you permission to continue on in your initiation ritual."

He is allowed to join.

"Thank you council," the young man begins to speak but he too is interrupted when the head elder nods his head, signaling the lycan down on the floor.

Acknowledging the nod, he grabs the potential by each arm and bites deep into his shoulder. His razor sharp teeth slice into the man's flesh with ease. The potential yells in agony. Blood flows from the wound and the droplets are quickly absorbed into the sandy floor. The new member does his best to tolerate the pain and accepts his initiation. With this savage act, the potential's life as a human ends and life as a Kingdom member begins.

Back in New Hampshire, in the warmth of the Professor's study, Anne snaps out of her daze as the Professor says, "Anne, it's getting late. You'd best be getting along. We wouldn't want to upset Rob."

She wearily looks down to her watch and panics.

"Oh my God, it's almost midnight. Professor, we need to get an alarm clock or something in here. The time just seems to fly by while we're working."

"Yes. Yes, it seems to, doesn't it," he responds.

Anne quickly runs about as she gathers her coat and bag. She grabs a handful of notebooks and shoves them into her bag. Once sorted, she stops at the doorway of the study.

"I think I've got everything. I'm off then, see you tomorrow Professor," she asks hastily.

The Professor pauses and looks to his watch.

"Anne, we've accomplished a lot this week. Let's take a break tomorrow. Spend some time with Rob and we'll resume on Thursday."

"Ok Professor, see you then. Good night."

"Good night, my dear."

# OVERWHELMED

So far, the two authors have put in over three months of work into the project, tirelessly working their way through each chapter. Both of them are occupying their usual places in the study. Anne is busy typing in some notes that the Professor had provided to her earlier.

The Professor is on the opposite side of the room going over some of the scrolls and artifacts laid out on the table.

Outside, the moon is full and the warmth of the spring day has yet to diminish into the night air. Unusual for the Professor, he has opted for few lights tonight. Aside from Anne's desk light, the only other light in the room is from the fire crackling in the fireplace and a few scattered candles about the room. There is an eerie quiet that is sporadically broken by the random keystrokes of Anne's typing.

After a few hours, she sits back in her chair to stretch her back. She turns her head from side to side and rubs the back of her neck with her hands. Checking the clock on her monitor she sees that it is 8:53.

Her attention then shifts to the Professor who is cradling something in his hands. Upon further investigation, she can see that it is a CD.

Waltzing over to the stereo, the Professor pushes a button that opens the CD tray.

He inserts the disk and announces, "Anne, I'd like you to listen to something."

This strikes Anne as peculiar because the Professor has never listened to music before while they worked. She thought to herself that this would be a nice change of pace, so she acknowledges in the affirmative.

"Ok."

He presses the Play button. The music is faint and rhythmic but Anne finds it to be very peaceful.

"That's not going to bother you will it, my dear," the Professor asks.

"No, no, it's fine. It's actually quite nice. What is it," she inquires.

"I was fortunate enough to be present at a re-creation of one of the Kingdom's ritualistic marriage ceremonies. This is some of the musical chants that go on during that ceremony."

"Wow, it's very captivating."

"Yes, I find so too," the Professor replies.

The music isn't overly loud, so it doesn't disturb them as they carry on with their work. Anne figures that the Professor needed it for inspiration as they had been working long hard hours recently. After an hour or so of inputting data, she finds herself glassy eyed and staring at the monitor. She shakes her head to help her snap out of her daze. It does little to help but she soldiers on and starts typing again. Suddenly, she feels a warm sensation course throughout her entire body. Her head feels dizzy and faint.

"Whoa," she says as she grabs the desk.

She turns from the desk and grabs her knees while staring at the floor. She closes and opens her eyes while lightly shaking her head. Nothing seems to work as the light-headedness persists.

Startled and concerned, the Professor rushes to her side, dropping to a knee beside her.

"Are you alright, my dear?"

"I don't know. I'm all of a sudden feeling a little light headed."

"Have you been drinking enough water? You know how you get."

"Yeah, I've got my water right here."

She reaches for her faded red water bottle on the desk to show the Professor.

"Anne, it's been a long day. Why don't you take a break? Drink some of your water and go relax on the couch for a few a minutes. I'll go to the kitchen and get a wet facecloth for your head."

Holding her by the elbow, the Professor helps her up and guides her around her desk over to one of the couches. As she lies down, he takes a seat on the coffee table to monitor her.

Anne assumes this dizziness is due to the fact that the two have been pushing long hours lately. As she lies back, she reaches for a pillow and slides it under her head. The rhythmic sounds of the CD continue to echo in the background. Her eyes close and she nearly falls asleep but she quickly snaps herself out of it. She sits up and takes a sip from her water bottle.

"Are you all right Anne?" he asks again.

Wary of causing a scene in her teacher's house and not willing to deal with the consequences of an already jealous boyfriend, she gives in to the notion her body might be telling her that it is time for her to go home.

"Professor, I hate to do this but maybe I should head home and get some sleep."

The Professor agrees with a nod. "Ok then, let's call it a night."

Anne pushes herself up off the couch and heads back to her desk. The Professor beats her there. He picks up her notebook and a few other belongings of hers and slides them all into her bag for her. Anne, meanwhile, guides herself toward the door while pulling on her sweater. She manages to make it only a few feet before she again gets light-headed and stumbles. Fortunately, the Professor catches her arm, preventing her from falling.

He suggests in a concerned tone, "I think I should drive you home tonight. I don't want you walking home like this."

She nods her head in agreement and replies, "Yeah, I think you're right."

But before she even gets to the hallway, she faints, collapsing on the floor.

"Anne!" he shouts.

The Professor tosses her book bag to the side and drops down beside her.

"Anne! Are you alright?" he shouts.

With Anne now lying completely unconscious on his floor, the Professor rolls up her jacket and places it under her head. He is growing more and more concerned as he tries to wake her but to no avail. Feeling her wrist and searching for a pulse, he finally finds the rhythmic pulse of her heart. He looks to his watch, checking for any abnormalities.

"Anne!" he yells in desperation one last time, but again to no avail. He quickly retrieves his cell phone from his pocket.

While unconscious Anne sinks into a deep dream state. She begins to experience vivid images swirling through her mind. Initially she finds herself standing in one of her old college classrooms that she spent many years in. She walks over to her desk and takes a seat. The roof above explodes outward, revealing a wondrous blue sky with dense puffy white clouds scattered about.

Images of her parents drift by and she feels warm and comfortable in this somnolent state. Floating all around her, more images from her past begin to appear.

Her attention is suddenly drawn to a vision of herself walking through the doorway. The figure walks toward her but appears to stare right through her. The apparition approaches Anne which makes her feel edgy and uncertain. The figure quickens its pace and comes right up to where Anne is. It absorbs into her and when this occurs Anne's body suddenly feels very empty and heavy. There is a sensation as if she is sinking. Unable to lift her arms or move, she panics and attempts to call for help. No sound comes out.

Her mind is frantic. The harder she breathes, the more panicked she becomes. More recent images of people begin to enter the room and Anne's eyes wildly scour over them hoping one of them will help her.

The Professor swirls past holding open a book. A vision of Rob and her running around the apartment, laughing and jumping on their couch calms her senses, but only for a moment.

The room grows very dark and the bright blue sky dissolves into night. Passages from their book can be heard all around as if the Professor were dictating them to her off in the distance.

The landscape evolves more quickly to violent scenes featuring what she perceives are lycans. The huge creatures are in a fierce battle with men. Other scenes of secret rituals the Professor had described appear before her. A group of Kingdom members, both men and women, wearing long flowing robes, enters the space around Anne. The men remove their robes revealing their naked, rugged frames but immediately transform into lycans. As the beasts make their way towards the women, who drop their robes exposing themselves to their partner, they as well transform into lycans. The lycans are double the size they were as humans. The males grab their partners around their wastes and engage in a rhythmic ritualistic act.

It starts out as intimate love making, but the setting changes again. Where it began as passionate, it now grows more aggressive and then into what appears to be a violent power struggle between the two creatures. They become ravenously connected with each other. Their claws and sharp teeth tear at each other's flesh as the pain that they each feel intensifies the act as a whole. The scene fills Anne with terror. The acts continue to swirl away and a light begins to pulse rapidly all around Anne.

Everything in the room grows dark and all the desks in the room drop away into oblivion. She feels very light as the seat she is sitting in falls away. Her body begins to float into a labyrinth of dreams. Her senses return as she touches down into a damp forest. She herself now engages in the scenes that her mind is creating.

Running feels like the obvious thing to do so she does. Trees and branches grab at her as she runs faster than she has ever run before. Her arms are irritated by all the small scratches and blood weeps from the larger cuts. Above her is a massive and brilliant full moon, brighter than any moon she has ever seen. It captivates her while clearing her mind of any prior issues. Then, the unexpected sound of wolves howling all around her doesn't startle her but energizes her spirit. She feels more alive than she ever has. The forest spins around her, the wolves continue to howl, and most surprising of all, she breaks her silence and lets out an epic howl as well. It just feels right for her to do so.

Then it all comes to an abrupt end when the Professor suddenly appears beside her. His calm expression stares at her for a split second and then he shouts, "Anne!"

Everything goes black.

The next morning, she awakens to find herself in her own bed. She sits up and feels her chest. The shirt she is wearing is damp from beads of sweat that are still rolling down her body.

"Rob?" she yells.

"I'm in the kitchen cooking breakfast," he replies.

She hears him clanging pots together and dropping silverware into the sink, followed by his booming footsteps marching down the hallway toward their room. He stops at the doorway to the bedroom.

"Holy shit, look at you."

"What happened," she asks.

"What happened?" he retorts. "What happened was, you passed out at the Professor's last night. After I pulled you out of his car and put you to bed, you proceeded to freak the fuck out, all night long. That's what happened. You must've had some dreams too because I've never seen you more vocal and restless while sleeping."

"That's so weird. All I remember is feeling woozy then bam. I did have these very weird dreams about you, the Professor and -"

She pauses, hesitant to reveal what she and the Professor are writing about.

"What," Rob asks.

"A bunch of it was about werewolves" she says reluctantly.

"Wait. What? Now that's weird. When was the last time we even saw a movie about werewolves?"

"I don't know, it was all very strange. Then next thing I know is a waking up here completely soaked."

She falls back to the mattress.

"Ow!" She reaches for her shoulder to discover that it is bandaged up.

"What happened here?" she asks.

"Apparently when you fell, you hit your shoulder on a sharp piece of furniture or something. The Professor said it wasn't bad but wrapped it anyway just to be safe. I don't know how bad it is. You were wrapped when you arrived. Check it out when you take a shower and make sure it's nothing serious. But anyhow, how are you feeling now?"

"Exhausted, like I didn't sleep at all."

"I'm not surprised," he continues. "When the Professor brought you home, oh by the way at 3AM, you were out like a light. I put you in bed, then you started moaning and acting pretty weird. I had to sleep out on the couch."

"Sorry babe, I really don't know what happened," she mutters back.

"Yeah, well I do. Too many goddamn nights up till 2 or 3 in the morning. It's too much and it stops now. For now on, no more working any later than midnight. Agreed?"

"Agreed. And honey, I'm sorry if I scared you."

"Anne, I understand what you guys are going through and you have this critical deadline to meet. But you can't be working until you pass out. That was some pretty scary shit last night. You need to get your shit back together. And I mean it. You can't be having any more episodes like last night. That was just friggin' ridiculous. I also think it's about time you got this checked out once and for all. I mean, not drinking enough water and getting dizzy because of it is one thing, but passing out is quite another."

"Rob, I was drinking water all night. You can ask the Professor."

"Yeah, well it was also stupidly late at night. You should have been home in bed by then," he retorts.

Anne reads Rob's tone and understands he's upset with her and the situation she caused.

"Ok hon, I'll make an appointment, just in case," she says.

"Thank you. Anyway, drink up."

He hands her a glass of orange juice.

"You're probably majorly dehydrated after all that sweating."

"I am, thanks," she responds while taking the glass from him.

"I'm gonna get you some aspirin and then finish making breakfast. Go shower up. It'll be ready in ten minutes."

He turns and makes it halfway down the hall before she breaks the silence, "Ok, dad," she says with a smirk.

Rob whips around irritated and ready to retaliate but stops short when he sees his fiancé sitting in bed looking at him with the biggest, warmest smile he has seen in a while. This is the reason he fell for her so many years ago, her ability to diffuse his temper with a look.

"So, you think my shit needs to be in order," she challenges.

"As a matter of fact-"

Anne interrupts him, "Then why don't you shut up and come show me."

She puts her arms up gesturing for him to come to her.

He grins, runs, and leaps for the bed. Landing on his knees, he gently drops on top of her.

His hands grab hold of her shirt, damp with sweat.

"Eww, gross," he protests.

"Shut up and be a man," she responds.

She wraps her arms and legs around him pulling him down to her. He doesn't resist as he lowers his head to her.

# AN ENDING AND A BEGINNING

Summer has arrived in Elm Hills. Flowers are in full bloom, expressing their bright, vivid colors. The trees and surrounding forests are full with leaves. The warm sun energizes everyone to head outdoors. The seasonal sparrows and warblers are back from their long winter flights. They dart about brilliantly searching for berries and insects to bring back to their nests. Locals start to manicure their lawns and up and down most every street in town. Housewives take to their mini gardens, planting flowers and colorful plants.

The summer also brings a conclusion to the school year and months of collaboration between the Professor and Anne. The two authors have successfully completed their book. It is on this day that the Professor gathered all the info the two have been working on and proudly shipped their completed manuscript to the publisher for printing.

To celebrate the books completion, Rob and Anne decide to have a quick and informal wedding. It is a very small gathering with only a few friends, and unfortunately for the prospering couple, an even smaller number of family members in attendance. Overcoming the loss of their parents were factors that had originally brought the two together. That was something that they eventually overcame together during their relationship. This same ideal had fostered the yearning for them to have a large family of their own.

The wedding was simple and quaint. The ceremony took place at the town park, where the couple stood in front of a white lattice arch covered with white roses. Their local pastor officiated the service with Christina as Anne's bridesmaid and Rob's only brother, Tom, flying in from Wyoming to be Rob's best man.

After the ceremony, the group convened at Durgin's. The couple had rented it for the day to enjoy some local food and music. Good friends of Anne and Rob, who had formed a band during their college days, offered to play at the couple's reception in exchange for food and the occasional draft. They also offered because they were beginning to enjoy some success in the area, and being able to add "Available for Weddings" would be a huge financial gain for them.

The wedding wasn't lavish but it was everything the couple had hoped for and they were extremely pleased to share the event with people close to them.

After most of the festivities had passed, the happy couple, sitting at the head table, decided to share some exciting news. Rob dings his champagne class a few times which quickly gets everyone's attention focused to him.

Rob stands up holding Anne's hand.

"Anne and I just wanted to thank everyone for making this the absolute best day of our lives. And before it ends we wanted to share some exciting news with you all." He pauses for dramatic affect and then states. "We wanted to let you know that Anne is pregnant and we are anxiously expecting our first child before the end of the year."

The crowd erupts in cheers and clapping. Several people approach the couple with handshakes and hugs as Anne blushes with gratitude. Christina who is sitting next to Anne elbows her in the ribs.

"How the heck did you manage to keep that from me," she asks.

"It was tough, believe me," she responds.

The two longtime friends hug to an array of flashes from eager picture-takers in the room.

To top off the celebration and as a "Thank You" to Anne for her help with the book, the Professor's wedding gift came as a complete shock. He knows the two couldn't afford to go on a proper honeymoon so he took it upon himself to help out. After the reception he confronts the newlyweds.

"Robert, Anne—I'm very proud of both of you," the Professor states. "And to show my appreciation for all the help that you, my dear, have given me, and to you Robert for putting up with our crazy schedules. I want you to accept this gift from me on this very special day. Robert, I understand that you have put in a great deal of effort to get your young business off the ground and that is something to be celebrated as well. So I give you this, with all my warm hearted thanks and good luck to both of you in the future."

The Professor hands over an envelope to Rob. Inside is an itinerary for a fully paid trip to Cape Cod for a week to enjoy a well-deserved honeymoon.

"Oh my God. Thank you Professor," Anne says.

"Yes, thank you sir. Thank you very much." Rob shakes the Professor's hand in gratitude.

"When is this for," Anne asks.

"Well my dear, your limo leaves tonight."

The Professor points to an awaiting limo out in the parking lot.

"You're kidding," Rob asks.

"Take it home and pack some things, then enjoy a nice ride to your destination."

Anne moves over to the Professor and gives him a big hug.

"Thank you Professor Caerwyn, for everything."

"It's my pleasure my dear. Now go and enjoy yourself. This night is about you two."

She turns to Rob after graciously accepting the gift. They head back to the reception while the guests are still dancing.

At the end of the night, they head off to the awaiting limo.

There aren't many better places to enjoy the summer more than in New Hampshire. It is ironic, though, at that very moment halfway across the globe in a place quite unlike New Hampshire, an email announces its arrival with a beep on a dusty computer It is well into the evening when Beauregard hears the message arrive. He resides in a lavish studio above The Geti Plains office. He is dressed in his customary white cotton outfit that allows him to deal with the sometimes intolerable temperatures of the passing day. Even now, hours after the sun has set, the heat from the day is still making its presence felt.

With a click of the mouse, he opens the email. It is from Krieger and it briefly states, "The book is done. What now?"

Beauregard slumps back into his office chair and brings his hand slowly up to his mouth while pondering the significance of the email. He tilts his head up and his intense gaze expands beyond the computer monitor out through the window behind it. A few minutes pass before his attention is drawn down to the telephone.

Still cupping his mouth, he presses the talk button with his other hand. A dial tone can be heard buzzing through the systems tiny speakers. He presses one of the quick dial buttons labeled thirteen. Beside it is simply written K.

After a moment of beeps, Beauregard finally hears the phone ring. Two more rings and the person on the other end picks up. The familiar sound of Krieger's rough, scratchy voice emanates on the other end.

"Ello?"

"Krieger? Beauregard here. I just got your email. Well done."

"Thanks, but like I wrote, what now?"

"Do nothing. Continue to keep an eye on the players. I want to know what the Professor does, and keep an eye on the girl as well just in case."

"The girl. Why? She's just a student of 'is?"

"Krieger," Beauregard retorts, "You of all people should know that sometimes things are not as they seem. I'm not saying she has anything to do with anything but you never know. The King may somehow use her as a pawn. Just keep an eye on her. That's all."

"Fine, she's local anyway. Shouldn't be 'ard to keep tabs on her. What about you? When will the great Beauregard be joining us 'ere to go over the final plans?"

"Reginald and I have a couple of more months here in Arusha, and a couple of odds and ends to tie up before we close up shop for the season. Beyond that I have set up several meetings with a half dozen or so clan leaders to make sure they are in agreement with the strategy moving forward. Once they are all in agreement, I'll head your way. It is going to be an excessive amount of travel tracking them down and getting timely meetings. Getting them all to agree will also be quite challenging. I wouldn't expect to see me until December at the earliest."

"What? Are you fuckin' serious? Me and the boys 'ave to sit around this piss hole of a town until December? Beauregard, this is going above and beyond. What the fuck are we s'posed to do until then," Krieger protests.

"Krieger, if we are not wary of the King's spies, then this is all for not. If the Kingdom suddenly learns of clans abruptly moving around, they might become suspicious and prepare for a threat. We need to move people around discreetly that won't draw any suspicion. Once the pawns are in place, then we strike. Unfortunately, this is going to take time and coordination."

"Also, might I remind you that you are over two hundred years old? It is only going to be a few months, so get a grip on yourself. This should seem like a vacation to you," Beauregard continued.

"Now, you have your instructions, keep an eye on the players and see if you can find anything else out. I don't want any surprises when I get there. And Krieger, don't you worry, dear friend, I'll be sure to contact you as soon as we've arrived in Boston."

"Can't wait," Krieger scoffs.

With an abrupt click, the line goes silent. Beauregard looks at the phone in displeasure, irked by Krieger's unpolished demeanor. He pushes the Talk button again to turn the phone off.

Crossing his arms, he continues to gaze out the window. Beside the window his personal armor is on display. The armor is polished to a bright finish, and the chest plate is adorned with the insignia of his clan. It is shaped like a traditional shield with three medieval style wolves in the upper right hand corner and a fleur-de-lis on the lower left. The two are separated by a diagonal stripe.

The armor itself is designed to be lightweight and to allow maximum mobility. The impressive steel protects the important parts—chest, shoulders, and upper arms while thick leather straps hold it all together. Lightweight chain-mail protects everything else, making the armor effective and formidable. Beside it stands a huge curved Arabian-style sword. It is polished and razor sharp.

The armor is impressive and it always gives Beauregard an immense feeling of pride whenever he views it. He stares at the armor for a bit then closes his eyes and drops his chin to his chest.

# KEEPING ORDER

A tall slender beauty walks along the sidewalk of a sleepy town in the mountains of Vermont. Her dress is unusual for this area. She is sporting tall black stilettos and a tight fitting leather outfit that accentuates her alluring form. Her long, flowing brunette hair is draped down around her shoulders and bounces ever so delicately as she moves. Her strut is slow and calculated, while there is a strong air of confidence in her facial expression. The early evening air is soothing across her face.

As she walks, there is a lot of activity in the neighborhood around her. Children and teenagers run around in wolf costumes trying to scare anyone they can. Young troublemakers throw rocks at houses as they run past. All about, the sound of breaking glass and people yelling and screaming can be heard. Small fires are scattered throughout the town as nervous homeowners struggle to maintain order around their properties.

Everywhere the woman looks is chaos. Another unusual feature about this town is the presence of bars on all the windows of all the homes. The scene might be normal for a suburb of Detroit or Los Angeles, but this is the middle of summer in a quaint New England setting.

The woman seems unfazed by all that is happening. Many of the boys certainly notice her as she passes but they take care not to upset the stunning beauty.

Further up the sidewalk, she happens upon a tall figure that steps out from behind a large maple tree in front of her. The stranger is wearing a black trench coat that has the collar pulled up, covering part of his face. The beauty stops in her tracks and reacts with a smile to the tall man.

"Well, howdy stranger," she remarks.

"Hello to you, my dear. Where can a man in town for the night find some fun for the evening," he asks.

"Well, if you're game for something daring, I have some friends who will show you the time of your life. Interested?"

"Absolutely, you can lead the way," he gestures to her.

He offers her his arm and she immediately loops hers through it. They walk side by side along the sidewalk.

"How long are you in town for, friend," she asks.

"Not long. I'm hoping to be on my way tomorrow. If you don't mind me asking, what is going on around here?"

"Well," she exclaims," this is the bright idea of our town leader, the Mayor. He is a big fan of Halloween, so he has proclaimed the 30th of every month to be Halloween. Except, of course, in February. That's when he goes on vacation. The only weird thing about these Halloween celebrations is that you are only allowed to dress up as a wolf. He's kind of eccentric and a little full of himself."

"Is he a friend of yours?"

"I guess. We used to date but that's been over with for a long time. I work for him now, but that's as far as that goes."

"It sounds like his position as Mayor has led him astray."

"I suppose."

"So, where are we going?" he persists.

"Funny you should ask. We are going to meet my friend, the Mayor."

"Oh really. Does this friend of yours have a name?" the tall man inquires.

"Full of questions, aren't you stranger? That's ok. His name is Patrick and you won't believe what he has in store for you, my handsome friend."

"You flatter. This meeting sounds risky. Should I be worried?"

She glances at the stranger with a gleam in her eyes that portends mischief.

"I don't know. You look like someone who can handle himself. Getting nervous?"

"No mum, there aren't too many things that make me nervous, especially not anything to do with Halloween."

"Well stranger, you and I are going to have fun tonight."

She clings to the man's arm and leans her head up against his shoulder as they make their way along the sidewalk.

Fifteen minutes later, they arrive at the center of town. It is eerily quiet though it looks as if a war has taken place here. Small trashcan fires burn everywhere. Several police cars are overturned and burned out.

"What the hell happened here?"

"Oh, just Patrick. Let's just say this is what happened during his election run.

Fortunately, he won. If he hadn't, I shudder to think what would have happened to this town."

"Where is he?" the stranger asks.

"Right over there."

She points to the town hall, the only structure that exhibits any sign of life. Loud music and strobes pulse out of most of the windows of the building.

"I'd like to meet him."

"Ok, let's go."

The two figures head across the town square to the main sidewalk leading to the town hall. She takes his hand and leads him up the walkway to the main door. He slows, pulling her to a stop. He looks intently at her then down to their hands. She takes note of his expression and realizes that her own nervousness has led her to grasp his hand very tightly.

Reassuringly she states, "Trust me, it's the only way you're getting in. Come on."

They continue up to the main door. Two heavyset men are somewhat standing guard at the door. As the couple approaches, one of them steps up to her.

"Bianca, nice to see you again. Who's this? Your latest love toy?" The guard chuckles at his own poor joke as he looks over to his partner who also smirks.

"Oh BJ, you are just so damn funny. He's a friend. I want him to meet Patrick."

"A friend, huh? Go ahead, but he better not cause any trouble."

Bianca pulls her companion through the door but before he makes it through, BJ chest bumps him hard into the door jam.

"Or I'm gonna have to kick the shit out him."

Bianca goes back and retrieves her gentleman friend by the arm and escorts him through the entrance. She then glares back at BJ and yells. "Why do you have to be such an asshole!"

BJ snorts as he giggles at the comment. "Just comes natural I guess."

The man fixes his hair and adjusts his coat as he stares down BJ. They move further into the building.

Techno trance music blares from speakers everywhere. There are hundreds of young people dancing and drinking anywhere there is space. Others, who have overindulged, are passed out along the walls and corridors of the main floor. The stench of stale beer is heavy in the main room and trash fills corners everywhere. Bianca leads the stranger up the main set of stairs, who witnesses a fight breaking out in one of the adjacent rooms. Eventually reaching the top of the stairs, they head down the main hall leading to a huge door with the title *MAYOR* stenciled across it.

She stops at the door and looks toward the stranger with a gleam in her eye.

"Here we are," she says with a smile as she turns the doorknob and pushes it open.

A powerful odor of hard liquor and drugs emanates from the room. The two take a moment before entering to get used to the overwhelming stench. The room is set up like a typical mayor's office except there's no desk. In its place is a long boardroom style table made of thick cherry wood. The room is washed in a red hue because the bulbs in the light fixtures have been changed from normal white bulbs to red-colored ones.

It is very dim and most of the young people occupying the room are in varying states of intoxication. Some are passed out on the floor while the remaining are enjoying themselves in various stages of undress. All of the girls sitting in the chairs surrounding the table are naked and are taking turns shooting heroin and smoking pot.

Bianca's companion keenly notices that all these young girls have sizable flesh wounds along their shoulders and necks. Blood that once flowed red from the wounds has now dried up hard and turned black over time.

Sitting at the end of the table and leaning back in a massive leather chair sits their host, Patrick. His legs are crossed while his feet, donning black leather Doc Martens, rest firmly on the end of the table. He is wearing tight fitting black leather pants and while not wearing a shirt, he is sporting an unusual bright red velvet robe. Sunglasses and an LA Kings baseball hat complete his unusual wardrobe ensemble. Patrick does reveal a fair amount of chest hair to go along with his long shoulder length hair. He is unshaven and completely unaware that he has two new guests.

Bianca and the stranger head over towards Patrick, carefully stepping over people passed out on the floor. When they reach the end of the table, Bianca beckons with her hand for the two girls sitting next to Patrick to leave. Bianca's stature here is obvious because the two girls do so without complaint. She and the stranger sit on opposite sides of the table with Patrick between them.

"Patrick," she calls loudly.

He turns his head slightly.

"Patrick," now a little louder.

There is still no response.

Bianca swipes his feet off the table and yells, "Patrick!"

The force of his feet dropping to the floor propels him forward forcing him to react.

"What the fu- who- what!" he yells.

He steadies himself against the table, tilts his head down and peers over his sunglasses at Bianca.

"Oh, it's you. What do you want Bianca?" he grumbles.

"I have someone I want you to meet. He is interested in seeing what we have going on here."

"Oh, really? And why should I give a shit?"

"Not that you would anyway but he does have something I know you're interested in and would be money."

Patrick looks at the tall man. "Oh yeah? You got some dough to spend?"

The stranger sits forward.

"I have some capital, if it can be invested wisely with a profitable outcome."

Patrick is clearly unimpressed with the man's vernacular.

"Invested? Look bub, either you're in or you're out. I trust Bianca has told you a little about our organization here and what it entails?"

"Oh yes, I am quite aware of all the rituals involved in joining your little club."

"Joining my little club? What I ought to do is smack the shit out of ya and take the money from your dead carcass."

Bianca steps up. "Patrick, we need him and his assets. Stop being a turd and realize that we could use a little help about now."

He looks back at her.

"You're sure about this guy?"

She nods in approval.

He looks back at the man.

"You're sure you wanna do this?"

The stranger nods back at him.

"Ok. Roll your sleeve up and give me your arm."

The man rolls up the sleeve of his trench coat exposing his forearm. Patrick grabs the sunglasses from his face and tosses them aside. He takes the man's arm and begins a slow transformation into a lycan beast. A snout extends from his face as his teeth elongate and protrude from the enlarging mouth line. The clever Mayor halts his transformation so his body stills retains most of its human form.

The stranger seems unfazed by the demonstration, as do many of the others in the room. Patrick holds the man's arm firmly and sinks his teeth deep into it.

"Aaargh!" Patrick shrieks. He stands up from the table and quickly reverts back to human. He frantically wipes the blood from his lips with both arms.

"What the hell? That is the most disgusting thing I've ever fucking tasted!" he shouts, spitting out the remaining blood from his mouth.

The stranger pulls a handkerchief from his pocket and wipes the blood from his arm. He then carefully wraps the wound with it all while glaring with an intense look of anger at his host. He slowly rolls down the sleeve of his trench coat and calmly states.

"That's because you've forgotten one very important rule. Lycans cannot convert someone who is already -" the man pauses.

Patrick looks at Bianca then back to the man.

"What?" he shouts.

"Lycan," the man finishes.

The statement causes Patrick to sober abruptly as the man before him rises to his feet. He removes his trench coat and places it on the table.

"Who are you, man," Patrick nervously asks.

The man smiles while he nonchalantly unbuttons his shirt revealing a leather breastplate with the Kingdom's crest etched in it. The Kingdom's crest is shield broken into four corners. The upper two corners have a wolf on each side holding a smaller shield down the middle.

Normally the lower two spaces have a fleur-de-lis on the left and the right side is vacant. But this one, Patrick realizes, is just a little bit different. That empty slot is occupied by a symbol that makes him very uneasy and that symbol that causes his concern is a crown.

The stranger rapidly transforms into one of the largest lycans that Patrick has ever seen. The massive beast towers over Patrick. The beast's claw grabs Patrick around the throat and raises him up high in the air until the two are face to face.

In a loud throaty tone, he yells, "I am your goddamn King!"

Patrick's velvet robe falls to the ground. The Wolf King looks down at it.

"Interesting choice of clothing, Patrick. Should I take any meaning from it?"

Terrified and barely able to breathe, he manages to talk.

"No. None your Highness."

"Are you sure, Patrick? A robe, and what's that, an LA Kings hat? That almost conveys a sordid status of King. Do you believe yourself a king, Patrick?"

"No, no, no sir. It's just a joke."

"Well, I will agree with you Patrick, it is a joke. This whole goddamn town is a joke!" the Wolf King yells as he heaves Patrick across the room, slamming hard into a bookcase then falling to the ground.

"What happened to you, Patrick? You had such great promise. Look at all this. Is this really the best you can do, laying siege to a country town and celebrating Halloween once a month?"

The King waits for any response fully knowing he won't get one. He continues.

"Real fucking clever, you imbecile! And who the hell do you think you are, foregoing the initiation process and converting humans yourself. What went wrong with you? You have no idea how disappointed I am with you."

Patrick clambers up on his hands and knees.

"I'm sorry, my King. Please don't give up on me."

The Wolf King looks around the room at all the people in it. Those that are awake are fixated on the King. Others are still passed out unaware what is taking place in the room. He storms over to Patrick again grabbing him by the throat. The King again raises him high above then pushing him hard against the wall.

"I'm sorry, Patrick. You have broken too many laws for me to excuse all this."

With one powerful squeeze, the King crushes Patrick's neck like an eggshell. He follows that with quick strike from his other hand, that shears Patrick's head clean off his body. Blood gushes from the torso as it drops to the ground. The decapitated head falls to the floor and rolls to a halt a few feet away. Blood from the head has spattered all over the walls and onto some of the girls in the room. The startling turn of events causes them to scream.

"Quiet!" the King shouts.

"Bianca."

"Yes, my King," she responds.

"You're in charge here. I want this mess cleaned up and I want it done quietly. Call the board for help. I want this town clean and I want there to be no trace of us ever being here. You've got one week. Anyone who has been converted must be sent to the sanctuary. If they don't comply then destroy them."

"Yes, sir."

"Bianca?"

"My King?" she replies.

"You've done well here. Your devotion to the Kingdom in this manner will be duly noted. I am proud of you. Now don't let me down in this endeavor."

"I won't my King, and thank you for believing in me."

"Oh, and Bianca?"

"Yes, my King."

"The one at the door. BJ I think his name was."

"Yes," she answers.

The Wolf King takes a moment to convert back to his human form.

He walks over to collect his trench coat from the floor. He throws each arm into it.

"Terminate him," he emphatically states.

"Yes my King. Right away," she responds.

He straightens out his clothing and exits the room, walking back down the hall and stairwell. His pace quickens as he leaves the building, but not before BJ drops to one knee and bows to his King as he passes.

# DELIVERY

Rob arrives home after receiving a particularly frantic phone call from Anne stating that she had started getting contractions, and that her water had just broke. Today is the day. When he pulls into the driveway, he sees Anne standing on the porch with her overnight bag in hand. She carefully waddles over to the car, opens the door, and falls butt first into the seat.

"Whew," she exclaims while she slides her legs in.

"Hi, babe," he says to her as he places her bag into the backseat.

"Hi." She buckles her seat belt around her large pregnant belly, "Ok I'm ready. Let's go."

Rob shifts the gear shift lever to reverse and backs the car out into the road.

It is near freezing out but because Rob's commute is so short, and even though the fan is blowing on high, the interior of the car hasn't warmed up yet. The trip to the hospital is even shorter, so they arrive only a few minutes later.

"Ugh," Anne groans. "The car was just getting warm."

"I know. At least the drive was short."

He parks the car out front of the emergency department where, fortunately for the couple, the hospital has valet parking. When he gets out, he hands the keys to the valet, who hands back a ticket to Rob. They walk in together and stop at the reception desk. Rob checks Anne in as a nurse helps her into a wheelchair. The registration clerk gives the nurse a room number and she whisks Anne away to her room.

A few moments later Rob finishes up with paperwork. He follows the directions to Anne's rooms. After a couple of wrong turns, he eventually meets up with his wife who is settling into her room. She has already changed into her hospital gown by the time he arrives and is sliding under the covers of her bed. The room is painted in a dark tan color and dimly lit.

There is a plant in the corner near the windows that are overlooking the parking lot. The uncomfortableness of her contractions as they become more intense is starting to show.

"Oh, I don't like that," she declares.

"What is it," he asks.

"It was just another contraction, but I gotta tell ya, they aren't anything like I thought they would be."

"Well, I'm here if you need me. Remember your breathing."

"Yup," she replies.

She does her best, breathing the way she was instructed in her birthing classes, to make the waves more tolerable. About ten minutes pass when things begin to get unusual. The contractions are coming more rapidly with each passing moment, and more ferociously than she would ever have thought.

"Rob!" she shouts.

He rubs her back and grasps her hand gently.

"I'm right here hon. What's going on?"

"I don't know. This doesn't seem right. This isn't what they said would happen."

"Dr. Shinto said the contractions would feel kinda crampy. This is like I'm being stabbed with hot daggers. Ugh!" she groans as another contraction hits her.

"It's ok, trust me. Do your breathing and I'm gonna go get the doctor."

He pokes his head out the door and beckons to the first nurse he sees.

"Nurse, somethings going on. Can you check on my wife, please?"

"Yes sir, I'll be right in," she says.

He rushes back to see that his wife has begun sweating a great deal but staying diligent with her breathing exercises.

The nurse enters the room and notices that Anne's face is telling a different story.

"Hi there, sweetie. Looks like you're starting to get uncomfortable. Let's see where you're at, ok? I'm gonna start by checking your blood pressure."

The nurse reaches above Anne and pulls a blood pressure cuff from the shelf behind Anne's bed. She wraps Anne's arm and squeezes the bulb to expand the cuff. While listening through her stethoscope, the puzzled look on her face gives Rob cause for concern.

"Is it ok?" he asks.

"It's a little high, but not unusual. I'm going to get Dr. Shinto just so he knows where she's at."

She looks to Anne, "Continue your breathing. You're doing great. I'll be right back."

The nurse leaves the room in a light jog.

"Uugh!" Anne growls.

"Rob, I know this is my first pregnancy, but this isn't going the way everyone described. There are sharp pains shooting down my legs."

"Hang in there babe, the doctor is on his way," he reassures her while rubbing her back.

The doctor finally gets to the room with the nurse in tow. His name is Dr. Shinto. He is an Asian man in his mid-fifties. Anne and Rob really feel lucky to have him because of his great bedside manner and infectious personality.

"Hey kids, how we doing," he asks in his usual upbeat manner.

"Aaaaaaaaaaaahhh!" Anne screams.

"Oh, that well. Alright. So Anne, the nurse tells me your blood pressure is a little high. That's unfortunate but it does fall in with what we talked about with you being hypertensive a few weeks back. I want to try and keep that under control so we're going to get an IV started and get some meds into you to lower those numbers."

The head nurse walks in behind them and the doctor quietly pulls her off to the side to speak with her. The other checks Anne's pressure again.

"I diagnosed gestational-hypertension two weeks ago and her BP is currently one fifty over ninety. That does concern me, so let's get the monitors set up, I don't want this progressing to pre-eclampsia. Get a drip going and start her on some nifediphine. Give Liz a call and tell her I may want to induce quickly. Have her get ready, now."

"Ok. I'm on it," she replies.

She hustles out the door. Moments later another nurse rushes in and rolls out a heart monitor from behind the bed. She untangles all the wires and begins to set it up.

"Doctor, BP is one sixty over ninety," the bedside nurse states.

The nurse with the heart monitor beckons to Rob.

"Sir, if you wouldn't mind, I need to slide in here to get this set up on her. Could you move to other side of the bed please," she asks.

"Sure," Rob sputters.

He moves around to the other side of the bed and reaches for Anne's hand while he rubs her shoulder.

Anne grimaces in pain. The doctor tries to calm her down.

"Anne, you need to try and relax somehow. We'll have the anesthesiologist here any moment to make you more comfortable but I need you to try and settle down a bit. Try breathing more slowly and deeply. It's going to come in waves. You need to try and manage it until she gets here," he explains.

"I'm trying Doctor, but the pain is absolutely unbearable," she pauses.

"Ugh-aaaaaaaaagh!" Anne screams.

The nurse monitoring her blood pressure places a cool, wet towel across Anne's forehead.

The other nurse finishes setting up the heart rate monitor and the first number it pings out is 124. When the doctor sees this, his intensity ratchets up.

"Damn it," he mutters to himself.

The head nurse returns and Dr. Shinto takes control.

"Alright people, lets induce her. I need Liz up here right now and I want the procedure room ready in case we have to go C-section. I don't want any more surprises," he shouts.

The head nurse leaves again and the other two nurses go to work setting up an IV and readying the room for the birth. Dr. Shinto moves beside Rob, who is losing color in his face.

"Rob," he says.

He turns to the doctor. "Yeah," he replies.

"Rob, look. Anne is going to be fine. Trust me on this. There is nothing she can throw at me that I can't handle," he says with a grin trying to calm the worried husband.

Anne's head drops back to the pillow as she lets out another scream. Everyone in the room turns to her. Her breathing is no longer measured but now very frantic. The heart rate monitor beeps at 134. Anne's eyes start to roll while she clenches her teeth in agony.

"She's seizing," the nurse yells.

Dr. Shinto runs to the bed and monitors her airway.

"Bite block, quickly. Let's go people, move," he shouts again.

The nurse runs over and inserts the block into her mouth. After about thirty-seconds the seizure subsides. The anesthesiologist, Liz, enters the room and immediately consults the doctor.

"What's going on," she asks.

"Hey Liz, she's pre-eclamptic. I want to induce right now before she or the baby have any more issues," he states.

"Doctor, one seventy-eight over one hundred," a nurse shouts.

Doctor Shinto leans over to Liz, grabs her arm, and whispers into her ear.

"Shit, Liz, we need to get the oxytocin going now or we're going to have to go cesarean," he states.

"I'm on it, just give me a second," she responds.

Liz sets up her box on a rolling cart beside the bed while the other nurses try to stabilize Anne. Beads of sweat drip down the side of her face. Her eyes are closed and her head is turning from side to side. She is mumbling and feeling very faint.

Liz finally calculates the appropriate dosage and feeds it into Anne's IV. Another nurse has Rob put on a gown in anticipation of the birth. He is stunned and his face is flush. His concerns for his wife and his future offspring are heightened.

Another contraction hits Anne and it is unbearable.

"Aaahhh, aaaahhhh, oh my god, oh my god, oh my god!" she yells.

Rob rushes to her side.

"Anne," he shouts.

A nurse switches towels on her forehead for a fresh one.

Anne opens her eyes as the contraction passes, but she is terrified.

"Rob, I can't see. I can't see! What's happening to me?"

Dr. Shinto reassures her. "Anne it's ok, it will pass, I promise you it's just a reaction of your blood pressure being so high."

Several of the nurses position Anne for birth and start monitoring her dilation. It typically takes only moments for the meds to start working but the nurses are stunned at Anne's progression.

"Doctor, she's crowning," one of the nurse states.

Dr. Shinto circles around to see that Anne is almost fully dilated and the baby's head is visible.

"Uh, ok then. Let's go, let's go!" he shouts. "This is happening right now, ladies."

Everyone takes their accustomed positions around the room preparing for the birth. Rob stands beside his beleaguered wife, rubbing her back.

"Oh no," she grunts.

"The baby is coming Anne. It won't be long, just another couple of pushes," he calmly states to her.

Anne tries to push but it is all too much for her frail body to tolerate. Her head drops back and she falls unconscious.

Dr. Shinto turns to the nurse next to him. "Go get Dr. Richardson. I'm going to need him."

"Right away doctor, "she replies.

The doctor and accompanying nurses work methodically as the baby is slowly worked out. When it finally pops free, a surge of blood follows.

"She's hemorrhaging," the doctor yells. "Contact the bank and get two units of O negative here immediately."

One nurse gently takes the baby from the doctor and wraps it in a cloth while the another nurse severs the placenta.

Anne is losing a great deal of blood. Rob sees the blood starting to seep around her waist.

"What is wrong with you? That man has done so much for us and you continue to be rude to him. You'd better get over it and start being nice to him. He hasn't done anything to you."

"It's just the way he talks. He makes me feel like an idiot."

"Rob, he's a professor of history. Compared to him you are an idiot-"

Rob looks up quickly, stunned at her remark but before he can say anything in retaliation, she continues.

"- and I'm an idiot too. He is a professor, after all, so get over it."

She cracks a smile as Rob sits down beside her. She reaches for the baby as he carefully passes Gabrielle over to her. Anne wraps her up in her blanket and settles down with her.

At that very moment Dr. Shinto checks in on the couple.

"Knock, knock," he cries out.

"Oh hey, Doc." Rob waves him into the room. Dr. Shinto is thin and athletic. His dark hair shows no sign of grey. Anne has stated many times that he could easily pass for someone half his age. He slides over to the end of Anne's bed and takes a seat.

"Hey, guys, how is everything going," he asks.

Anne replies, "It's going well. I did manage to finally get her to feed a little bit ago."

"Good, good. Keep at it."

He puts on his glasses that are hanging around his neck and examines some charts on a clipboard he brought in with him.

"Well, I've got a couple of things for you. As you both know, this was a trying delivery to say the least. I had a chance to look at your last set of ultrasounds with some of the other doctors and we went over your current charts. We all came to the same conclusion that you should be fine. We didn't see anything that alarmed us or that might indicate any future problems. So you both can eliminate any need for concern. The worst should be behind us."

"That's great news, Doc," Rob says.

"I just recommend that you get as much rest as possible and take it very easy for a couple of weeks. That means no marathons or bull riding," he says with a smile.

"Ok, I'll try," Anne giggles.

"I'm also going to suggest a slightly longer stay here than we would normally recommend just so we can keep an eye on you and make sure everything heals properly. Beyond that, we obviously want to see you on your normal six-week checkup just to make sure you and baby Gabby are continuing to do well. Rob, I'm gonna ask that she rely heavily on you for at least for a couple of weeks."

"Will do, Doc." Rob replies.

"Jesus, Rob, what are you, Bugs Bunny?" Anne interrupts.

Dr. Shinto laughs.

"No, no, don't worry about it. It's actually a nice change from everyone being so formal around here. I wish more people would call me Doc. I think it lightens the mood."

Rob looks around and is still confused by Anne's remark.

"But I digress," Dr. Shinto continues. "You know what to do and what I don't want you to do. Other than that, enjoy Gabrielle and if you need anything, give a ring."

"Thank you, Doctor. That is a huge relief. Thanks for everything," replies Anne.

"You bet guys. I'll check in on you a little later. Get some lunch in you."

"We will and thanks again for everything," Anne replies.

Dr. Shinto smiles and is out the door in a rush.

"Well, that's good," says Rob.

"Yup. Looks like this little girl will have a baby brother or sister in her future after all."

Rob looks at Anne and replies, "Well, if you're up to it, so am I."

"Let's see how we do with this one first, idiot!"

Anne starts giggling as Rob puts his hands up twiddling his fingers as if threatening to tickle her.

"You punk! You better not!" she shouts.

"You better believe I would," he exclaims.

"No Rob, don't! Ow, ow, ow," she grabs her stomach uncomfortably.

Just then, another voice is heard from the couple's doorway.

"Ah-hem."

Christina is standing in the doorway in tight fitting ski pants and a ski jacket. She is also carrying an armload of flowers and a bundle of balloons. The sight of her BFF gets the best of Anne's emotions and she begins to tear up.

"Hey, you, get your butt in here," she beckons.

"Yay," Christina utters as she hustles into the room.

She hands Rob the flowers and then delivers a big hug to her best friend. After a long embrace she turns back to Rob and greets him with a hug and a quick kiss on the cheek.

Christina's smile is infectious and even Rob is happy to see her.

"How are you doing, you big lug," she asks.

"I won't lie, it was a little unnerving but we all pulled through," he replies.

"Yeah, I know. Everyone at Durgins's heard about it and we were all freakin' out. I'm glad. We're all glad you're ok."

"Thanks sweetie," says Anne.

"Hey, before I forget, you know those three scumbags we see around town from time to time?"

"Yeah," replies Anne.

"Well, they were hanging outside of the parking lot as I drove in. I swear they were watching me the whole time."

"That's weird," Anne replies, "I see those guys everywhere. What's their deal?"

"I dunno. I think they work over at Smitty's, you know, the tow truck place. I think they sell a little too."

"What, drugs?"

"Duh. Yeah stupid. You remember my old boyfriend Jimmy. I think he used to buy pot from them back in the day. I'm sure they're probably into more than that now."

"Next time I see them, I'm definitely calling the cops. They're always such assholes and you be careful when you leave," Anne warns.

"Totally. Anyhow, let me meet the little monster that I hear has been causing all this trouble."

"Well, this is she. Auntie Christina, I'd like you to meet Gabrielle."

Anne lifts Gabby up so Christina can hold her. Christina takes the baby and cuddles her tight.

"Oh my God, she is so friggin' cute. Auntie is going to spoil you like you wouldn't believe."

She smells the top of Gabrielle's head while gently rocking her in her arms.

"Mmm, don't you just love that new baby smell?"

She looks down to the baby again and rubs noses with her.

"Oh my God you guys, I can't believe how cute she is. I can't take it. If you ever need a babysitter, you know who to call."

"We appreciate that Chris. Who is it?" Rob remarks.

Christina turns to Rob, swiftly elbows him in the ribs, leans over, and whispers to him.

"Asshole."

She looks back at Anne.

"How are you doing, hon?"

"I'm good, everything is fine. They're going to keep me here a little longer just for observation, but I'm good. The doctor says everything is fine."

"Awesome. Like I said, everyone at Durgin's was so worried when we heard the news."

"Well, thank them for me and be sure to tell them I'll be in as soon as I can."

Outside the cold temperature continues to test the mettle of the small community, but inside this one room of the hospital, the weather isn't affecting the emotions of these two proud new parents.

# CHANGES

It has been a busy six weeks for the young couple. Rob's graphic design business has been seeing a steady rise in new clients. The checks from the book keep coming in at a consistent pace and the amounts are much bigger than Anne had ever expected.

Gabrielle has been a picture of health and a blessing to the couple although the addition of Gabby to their family has made for very tight quarters in their downtown duplex. Out of necessity, Anne hire's a real estate agent to help the couple find a new home.

Today, Anne has arrived at Dr. Shinto's office as directed for her first postpartum checkup. Rob has taken Gabrielle for the day so Anne could visit without distraction. She is seated in a waiting room that is brightly lit and warm. That's what Anne really appreciates about Dr. Shinto's office. He goes out of his way to make sure his offices as well as his patients are comfortable. Many other doctors' offices tend to be cold and uninviting.

The nurse eventually calls Anne's name and leads her to an exam room. She only has time to hang her coat before a light knock on the door indicates the doctor's arrival.

"Knock, knock," he says.

Anne now thinks that is his entrance catch phrase.

"Good morning, Dr. Shinto," Anne replies as she steps back and hops up onto the exam table.

"Hey, Anne. Wow, look at you. You look great."

"Why, thank you. Looks like you're having a good day."

"I am, thank you."

The doctor drops his notebook on the countertop and sits on a rolling stool. He rolls over to her and greets her with a pleasant smile.

"So Anne, how are you? How is everything going with little Gabby?"

"Things are going great actually. I thought I would still be feeling some affects but I don't. I really feel energized and good."

"That's excellent. How about everyone else," he asks.

"Well, Rob couldn't be happier and Gabby is the absolute best baby. She sleeps through most of the night and is very intuitive when awake. We got lucky with this one, I think."

"Well, take some of the credit. You'll find a lot of that comes from great parenting and great genes. You and Rob keep up the good work. So you're feeling ok? Everything seem to be ok with you in general?"

Anne pauses for a second and begins. "Well, I have had some peculiar things happening lately."

"Really, like what?" Dr. Shinto asks.

"Well, I've had these crazy night sweats. Not all the time but maybe a couple of times a week. And on those nights, I don't sleep well at all. I kind of reasoned with myself that it was just my body trying to get back to normal, but I don't know," she shrugs The doctor quickly responds, "It is possible you might have a slight case of postpartum depression. That's not uncommon and nothing to worry about. Anything else?"

"Rob has also stated on numerous occasions that I've had some pretty rugged mood swings as well."

"Totally natural and your concerns are understandable. Your body went through a long and ultimately demanding pregnancy. It just needs a little more time to recoup. I'll tell you what I'm going to do. We'll do the normal vaginal exam and then we'll follow that up with some blood work. What we'll probably end up doing is get you on some mild anti-depressants just to take the edge off. We will then follow that up with another visit in about two months to see how they're working. If all goes well, at that point we'll gradually wean you off of them. How's that sound?"

"Doc, anything that will allow me to get a good night's sleep, I'm all for."

"Anne, nothing you're describing is unusual for a new mother. We'll tweak you a little bit with some meds and then go from there. Sound good?" he asks.

"Sounds good to me," she replies.

"Alrighty, let's get started."

At that same time, Christina has just finished up her shift at Durgin's. She starts her walk home, taking her usual route through the park, then down a trail to the other side of town where her apartment is. This time however, she is met with some unexpected guests.

Krieger and his two cohorts emerge from some bushes and block Christina's way.

"'Ello, 'ello miss," Krieger says.

Startled, Christina stops and takes a step back.

"Still doing the accent, huh? What do you assholes want," she defiantly states.

Inn's limited patience is already exceeded, so he rushes over, grabs her by the face and pushes her to the ground.

"Learn your place, bitch," he yells.

"Inns!" Krieger shouts.

Inns looks back, then reluctantly takes his place behind Krieger.

"You're not done yet," he says to Christina.

"What?"

"I said, you're not done yet. You still ave' work to do."

Christina gets up and dusts herself off.

"Look, we all want the same thing here. Why are you guys being such fucking dicks?"

Krieger turns to his friends, shakes his head, and smiles.

"That's funny," he says as he swings around to give Christina a powerful backhand to her face that sends her staggering to the ground.

She touches her face in pain and tears start to stream down her cheeks.

Krieger points at Christina.

"You and your kind 'aven't got a chance. Finish your job and you won't be seeing us again."

"Alright, alright. Now fucking leave me alone," Christina shouts in disgust.

Krieger pauses, satisfied that she has understood his message. He turns and leads the others back down a side trail.

Christina gets up again and walks over to where her bag is lying. She bends over and swipes at it frustrated. She turns and looks in the direction of where they went and mumbles under her breath. "Assholes."

She pulls a napkin from her jacket pocket and gently wipes the blood from her now swollen lip.

Anne's visit lasts about thirty minutes. After her exam, she gets into her car and drives towards home when her cell phone rings. She reaches into her purse, which is on the passenger side seat and feels around until she finds it. She hastily slides her finger across it to answer before it goes to voicemail.

"Hello?"

"Anne, it's me. Christina."

"Hi hon, what's up?"

"It's those three assholes again."

"What happened?"

"I was cutting through that trail behind the park going home."

"Yeah?" Anne responds.

"Well, those creeps came out of nowhere and knocked me to the ground. They started asking all these questions about you. How do they know you?" Christina asks.

"I don't know. But what about you. Are you ok?"

"I have some scuffed elbows and my jacket is dirty, but I'm fine. Something must have spooked them because they left fairly quickly after rapid firing a bunch of questions at me. After that, they just ran off into the woods. They didn't even wait for any answers. Anne, what gives? Why are they so interested in you?"

"Christina, I have no idea what their deal is. Where are you now," she asks.

"I just got home."

"Alright, I'm just leaving the doctor's office now. I'll be over in ten minutes, ok?"

"Ok, but Anne, please be careful. They still might be hanging around and I don't want you to get hurt."

"I'll be careful. Be there soon."

Anne slides her finger over her phone ending the call. Another swipe and she dials Rob's number.

"Hey hon, what's up?" Rob answers.

"Rob, Christina was just attacked by those three guys we've been seeing around."

"What? Is she ok?"

"Yeah, she says she's fine but I'm headed over there now. She said they were asking about me."

"You? Why?"

"I don't know. I'll know more when I get there. I'll probably call the cops when I get there just to file a report."

"Ok, be careful. I'll be here if you need anything. If not, I'll see you when you get home," he says.

"Alright, see you then. I love you."

"I love you too," replies Rob.

Anne tosses her phone into her purse and pulls over to the side of the road, waiting for cars behind her to pass. Once they pass, she turns the car around and drives to Christina's apartment to check on her best friend.

About ten minutes later she arrives at the apartment. She runs up the stairs and in one motion, knocks on the door while pushing it open. Upon entering Anne sees her friend dabbing the side of her mouth with a wet paper towel.

"Oh sweetie, are you ok?" Anne asks.

"Yeah fine. Nothing an icepack and a six pack won't fix," Christina replies.

"What did they want?"

"I dunno, maybe I still owe them some money from some pot I bought a while ago."

"But you said they were asking about me. What were they asking?"

"I'm not really sure, it all happened so fast. I think they were just trying to scare me. You know, all Tony Soprano like. If you don't pay up we're going to go visit your friend and take it out of her type of thing," she chuckles.

"Christina, this is serious."

"Look, it was nothing. I'll take care of it. Tomorrow I'll go to the cops and file a report with Rick and that'll be the end of it. You know Rick, he doesn't take any shit. He'll track them down and kick the shit out of 'em."

Anne looks to her and ponders for a moment.

"Alright, you promise you'll go to the cops?"

"Yes for Christ's sake, I will."

"Fine. What can I do for you? You need some ice?" Anne asks.

"Well I could really use a hug," Christina states with an exaggerated sad face.

"Aw." Anne walks to Christina and wraps her arms around her, hoping the small gesture will comfort her.

It does.

# A NEW HOME

Several weeks after Christina's attack on a particularly warm day in April, Anne and Rob are standing in the driveway of a very modest house on the outskirts of town. Anne is holding Gabrielle in her arms as they wait for their real estate agent, Jan, to arrive.

"Anne, this house looks awesome but I'm still not sure how the heck we can afford this."

"Look, you need to get over this. I've explained it to you a million times. Your business has been very consistent and you're getting a lot of repeat business. Along with the money from the book, this really will be no problem for us to afford. You have to trust me on this that the numbers work. Besides, you've been working very hard. Give yourself some credit, you deserve this."

"If you say so. You're the money queen."

Just then, the unmistakable sputtering of Jan's car can be heard off in the distance.

"That's got to be her," remarks Rob.

To neither one of their surprise, Jan's beat up old minivan crests the hill and pulls into the driveway. The engine stops with a stutter and out steps Jan.

"Hey, you two. Sorry I'm late."

"No worries, Jan. Looks like I see a new dent and another hubcap is missing," Rob quips.

"Ha, ha, very funny. For your information, that ice cream truck never signaled. That one wasn't my fault."

Rob leans over to Anne and whispers, "Jeez, I was only kidding."

Anne elbows him in the ribs. Jan retrieves her briefcase from the back of her van and asks the obvious question of Rob.

"Ok you, Mr. Rob. I've already made the mistake of getting out of the car. Let's not waste anyone's time here. Am I getting back into my car?"

"Well, Jan, I think you may have finally found it. This may be the one," he gratefully answers.

Jan puts her hand to her chest and looks at Anne with a big smile.

"Are you serious?" she asks.

"Yup, I think this one's a keeper," he replies.

"Hallelujah! Anne, I think we may have finally won."

"Well, we both knew he was very particular," Anne replies.

"Let's go inside and take a look before he changes his mind," Jan urges.

They all walk towards the front door but a sudden greeting surprises them.

"Hello there," shouts a man from the other side of the fence by the driveway.

"Are you two thinking about buying this place? You couldn't have made a wiser choice."

Rob stops and beckons to Anne. "You go ahead inside. I'll be there in a sec."

He jogs over to the man and introduces himself.

"Hi, how you doing? I'm Rob. Rob Neely and that's my wife Anne."

The man is a tall, well-built black man sporting a military style flat top. Rob guesses him to be in his mid-forties and his posture is so tight, Rob is sure he came from a military background. His old faded carpenter's jeans and white tee-shirt were soiled from dirt and sweat, clues that he must have been working in the flower garden along the fence prior to their arrival.

Rob presses his hand forward and is met with a surprisingly firm handshake. When the man speaks, he carries a slight southern tone that is not typical to New England.

"Pleasure to meet you Rob. I'm Leon. Whatever you want to know about this house, just ask. By the way, did your realtor tell you about the property values here? They're the best in the state."

"Really?"

"Oh, yes…a lot of folks trying to get into these parts. My wife Stephanie and I have lived here for nearly sixteen years. It's quiet, private, and absolutely beautiful. The best parts about living here, aside from the property values, are the woods out back."

"What about -"

Leon interrupts, "They are conservation lands. There are thousands of acres back there for biking, hiking, whatever you want."

"No kiddin."

"Oh yeah. You are guaranteed never to have a neighbor behind you. Absolute privacy."

"That's -"

"Great, ya know, for property values. Why don't you buy this house? Steph and I and the other neighbors cross the way there have been waiting for quite some time for the right people to buy this place and you two look pretty upstanding."

"Well, we -"

"You keep the lawn cut?"

"Well, yeah -"

"Good, how 'bout your wife, does she run?"

"Yeah, she loves -"

"Good, my wife has been trying to get Louise over there to run but she ain't into it as much. So, she needs a partner. You keep that lawn cut, property values you know, and you'll love it here. Well, I gotta go fertilize. You got any questions, feel free to hit me up. Nice to meet-cha, Rob."

Leon shakes Rob's hand, turns with a slight hand wave over his head as he disappears into his garage.

"Yeah, nice meeting you too, and thanks," Rob says, finally getting a chance to finish a sentence.

He jogs up to the open front door of the house. Once he gets a couple of steps in, he is awestruck at how beautiful the interior of the house is. Everything is modern and convenient but surprisingly warm with rustic earth tones throughout.

"Rob," Anne runs over to him, "this place is unbelievable."

"Yeah. It certainly is." Rob looks all around and then questions, "Jan, why hasn't this sold yet?"

"Well, to be honest, I'm the only one the owner allows to show it, also I'm good friends with Steph and Leon, whom I assume you just met, and Jack and Louise are across the road. So, I really wanted to make sure I got the right people in here, and I think that you two will make a good fit."

"Knock, knock. May we come in?" a female voice hollers from outside.

"Yes, come on in ladies," Jan shouts in reply.

In walk two women who also appear to be in their early forties. They both are all smiles and full of excitement. Jan introduces the two women.

"Rob, Anne, this is Stephanie, Leon's wife and this is Louise. Louise and her husband, Jack live across the street."

Stephanie is a tall black woman with a very slender and fit physique. Her black hair is medium length and pulled back into a ponytail and she is wearing dark, blue spandex running pants with a grey sweatshirt. She, like Leon, has a slight southern accent.

Louise is slightly shorter, wearing faded jeans and a tan blouse. She is a little over weight but has strong Italian features that make her very attractive for her age.

Anne steps up. "How nice to meet you ladies."

"Nice to meet you too. Janet has told us a lot about you. Now, before we go any further, you are going to buy this house, right? I mean isn't it just absolutely charming?" Steph inquires.

"Well, so far Rob and I love it."

"Oh, and isn't she just a charming little angel," Louise exclaims pointing to Gabrielle. "How old is she?"

"She's almost five months and a little tired," Anne replies.

"She is precious," Louise continues.

"Thank you."

"Do you run?" asks Steph.

"Yes, I love running but I don't get to go very often because of my schedule and well, now this," Anne holds Gabrielle up a little higher.

"Nonsense. I need a partner to push me, and Louise isn't that person."

Louise interrupts. "Now don't you start that again," pointing to Steph. "What she means is, I will be happy to baby-sit while you go run with her. It'll get her off my back and I love children, so don't you hesitate to ask."

"That is very sweet of you. Thank you both," Anne responds. She looks over at Rob and asks, "Well what do you think?"

"What do I think?" Rob responds.

He gives a quick look around, hastily surveying all that he can from his vantage point. Everything is new and clean. He moves into the kitchen and marvels at the modern appliances. Flicking the water faucet on then off, he turns to the gathering around him.

"Jan, this one has three bedrooms and two and a half baths right?"

"Yes, that is correct. Plus, an attic space for storage and a full unfinished basement, ready for whatever you want to do with it."

"I see, then. Well, I guess—I think this is our new house."

"Yay!" both women scream as they clap their hands and jump. It has been a long time since this home has been occupied and their excitement gets the best of them.

"You two, oops, I mean three will just love it here. Welcome to the neighborhood," Steph declares.

The two women skip over and hug Rob, Anne, and Jan.

"Now, if you two need any help moving, you just let us know. Jack and Leon got nothing better to do these days," Louise offers.

"I appreciate that. We'll let you know," Rob replies.

Jan interrupts, "Hey Anne, why don't you and Rob go check out the rest of the place and make sure everything is where it's supposed to be."

"That's a good idea," Steph says. "You two look around. Remember, if you need anything, you let us know. Janet has our phone numbers."

Steph grabs Louise by the arm.

"Thank you very much, we will," replies Anne.

The two women exit through the front door giddy with excitement. Janet heads upstairs as the young couple follows close behind.

# A MEETING

Krieger, Inns, and Malachai stand alongside a building that is closed up for the night. Hidden from sight they hunker in the shadows of a solitary light shining over the neighboring parking lot. A silver BMW sedan pulls into the lot and slowly glides toward the three men. The headlights illuminate the trio as it rolls to a stop in front of them. One of the back windows rolls down.

Krieger snickers as he saunters up to the open window. He can see that Reggie is at the wheel and Beauregard is sitting comfortably in the back.

"You always did 'ave a flare for presentation, Beauregard. Not that I care, but 'ow was your trip," he asks snidely.

"The trip was fine Krieger. Has there been anything new to report?"

"Well, as you know, the book is done and 'as been done for some time. Other than that, no, there is nothing new to report. You mind telling me what the 'ell is going on? If I'm not mistaken, this damn truce 'as been over forever and it's been months since we've last spoken. I want to know what you and your people 'ave been doing all this time," Krieger states in an aggravated tone.

"Whoa, whoa, whoa. Calm yourself, my old friend."

"Don't you tell me to calm myself," Krieger responds abruptly. "My people have been in place all this time and they are growing impatient. It is time to put our plan in motion. If the King or anyone else finds out what we're doin', this could all be for nothing."

"Patience, Krieger. The final parts of the plan have been finalized and right now, the more info we have, the greater the chance for success."

Krieger never liked Beauregard and is easily irritated by his polished demeanor. He raises his voice and gets more animated at the thought of further delay.

"Look, B," Krieger calls Beauregard B because he knows how much it annoys him, "'ow much time do you want to give 'im? Eventually, the King will find out what we're doing and counter it. What if, for instance, while we're waiting 'e 'as a kid? How much would that screw everything up? We can't continue to just sit around. It's time to move."

"An heir you say?" Beauregard interrupts. "Funny that you should mention that because that very circumstance, I fear, may already have occurred."

"What? Bullshit! I 'aven't heard anything of a kid," Krieger scoffs.

"My spies tell me there are rumors of a child," Beauregard adds.

"See, this is what 'appens!" Krieger spouts.

"Not to worry Krieger. We have been planning for just this situation should the rumor be true. That is the reason for the delay. All you need to concentrate on is one simple thing. If there is no heir, then there can be no heir to the throne. Correct?" Beauregard asks.

"Yeah, that's true, it just adds more strain to an already tricky task. The heir will be hard enough to find, but finding and eliminating it, that will be difficult to pull off," Krieger responds.

"Leave that to me. You just do your best to confirm the rumor and where they might be hiding the child. Then we shall go from there. What about the girl, this Anne I've been hearing about?"

"She's useless and a dead end. She lives in the outskirts with her 'usband and 'asn't 'ad any contact with anyone. Caerwyn just used her to help write the book and that's it. He 'asn't even spoken to her since they finished the book. We still mess with 'er from time to time, just to get 'er panties in a bunch."

"I would still like to meet her. She might know something and not even be aware of it."

"Whatever. But don't push me Beauregard. My clan is growing agitated by your delays."

"Don't worry, my brother. After all is done, you and your clan will get what you are owed."

Beauregard pushes a button on his door panel and his window goes up.

Krieger is outraged at Beauregard's deliberately curt ending to their conversation. He would love nothing more than to put his fist through the window and put an end to Beauregard. But he knows right now they need each other. Neither of their clans is strong enough to go against the King's army.

Reggie shifts the gear lever into reverse and the BMW backs up into the vast parking lot. The three men back away from the car as it moves toward the street.

Reggie gets very annoyed when in the presence of people from other clans. He loves his pack and wants only the best for it.

He looks up into the mirror and murmurs, "Excuse me sir."

Yes, Reggie, what is it?"

"The plan is still to use Krieger's clan to help overthrow the King, right? You're not really going to allow him or his deplorable pack any part of the throne or the assets behind it?"

"My dear Reggie, you know me better than that. As I told you before, once Krieger has outlived his usefulness, then he will no longer live. Without a leader, his clan will be disoriented and will be easily recruited. The best use I can think of for them to be matriculated into our army."

"Right sir. Excellent plan, sir. Sorry to question."

"That's quite alright, Reggie. Remember, there are no absurd questions, only absurd clan leaders."

"Oh, right sir. Quite right."

Krieger and his two affiliates disappear back into the shadows. Reggie spins the steering wheel right as the sedan rolls off into the night.

# UNEXPECTED GUEST

The next day, Reggie wields the big BMW down the main street towards the university. Beauregard has plans to meet with the Professor for an unannounced meeting. Reggie guides the car through a tight parking lot, stopping by the sidewalk in front of the Professor's building. Beauregard exits the vehicle and leans back in.

"Fifteen minutes, Reggie."

"Yes sir," the servant replies.

Reggie drives away. The path up to the building is quite long and it takes Beauregard a few minutes before he arrives at the stairs to the front entrance. Today is an off day so the students are away and the classrooms are empty.

Beauregard enters the through the heavy front doors and is in awe of how pristine the marble floors are. The shine is impressive and he almost feels a bit guilty walking over it.

Nevertheless, he proceeds down the main corridor of the school. The sound of his polished wingtips hitting the floor echo off the walls.

He eventually reaches the Professor's classroom where he pauses at the doorway. He peers into the room to see the scholar writing on the blackboard with one hand while referring to a thick history book that he is holding in the other.

Sensing the visitor, the Professor looks over his shoulder slightly to identify his guest.

"Ah, Beauregard, what a surprise. I've been wondering when to expect you?"

Beauregard has always made the Professor nervous but he greets him with as much warmth as he can muster.

"I got my copy of the book. Very well done, Robert. Very well done indeed. Did my scrolls help?" he asks.

"Yes, very much indeed, thank you. You'll be happy to know that copies of the book have been distributed to all the clans. There now exists a complete historical documentation of the Kingdom and of the clans. Everyone will have an accurate, documented heritage that can be passed on to future generations. No doubt, I assume you'll be using it for recruiting?"

"Very funny, Robert. Like you, my heritage is very important to me. I relished the idea of working with you and exchanging ideas with someone as intellectual as yourself. You have no idea what a privilege it was for me to get the opportunity to work with you on this project. It was a nice change. But I digress. You know why I'm here?"

"Yes, yes. I've saved it for you, assuming you would eventually come looking."

The Professor walks over towards his desk, reaches into his pants pocket and pulls out his set of keys. He unlocks the lower drawer, slides it open and retrieves a large envelope that is thick with money.

"Here you are."

He tosses it towards Beauregard who snags it in mid-air.

"By the way, how are things going in Africa these days," the Professor asks.

"Exhilarating. Oh, and by the by, any news about a possible heir to the throne?"

Beauregard replies abruptly.

The mood in the room quickly turns tense as the Professor turns and looks at Beauregard sternly.

"No, not to my knowledge. Why do you ask?"

"No reason. It's just that I've heard news to the contrary."

"Well, I have not and if I did, you know I wouldn't have any interest in telling you."

"Ah, Robert, no need to be like that. We are all brothers in this world."

Beauregard slowly makes his way over to the blackboard and examines the Professor's notes.

"Can't two great minds like ourselves enjoy this momentary peace that this book has brought?"

"You're referring to the truce? Don't play me for a fool, Beauregard. You know as well as I, now that this book is done, the truce is over."

"Robert, please. I assure you I am here in peace. I'm just visiting an old friend and have no intentions of starting any trouble. Speaking of the book, tell me about this co-author Anne. I've read enough of your work to know that you didn't write most of this."

"She was one of my brightest students a couple of years back. She has a wonderful talent for writing. I thought she would be a great asset to have in writing the book."

"Indeed she was." Beauregard nods as he picks up a piece of chalk and adds a comma that was missing from a sentence on the chalkboard.

"So, where is she now?" he continues.

"I haven't seen her since we finished the book. I've talked to her a couple of times but she's very busy these days. I'm not sure what she's been up to lately. Like I said, I haven't seen her in quite some time."

"I see. So, tell me Robert, did she know where you got most of the information and artifacts?"

"I told her I got them from collectors."

"Interesting. I think I should like to meet her someday and thank her personally," Beauregard adds while waving the envelope. He moves away toward the door.

"You leave her alone. She's an innocent girl who doesn't need to get involved in any of this," the Professor protests.

"Yes, anyhow, Robert, I bid you good day. It was nice to see you again. I would love to collaborate with you on something else somewhere down the road. Or maybe just to catch up over tea from time to time."

"Perhaps," the Professor replies. "Good day to you, Beauregard."

Beauregard turns and nonchalantly exits the room refusing to respond to the Professor.

The Professor looks at the empty doorway listening as Beauregard's footsteps grow fainter the farther he walks down the hall. He looks down at the open drawer at his desk.

"No, don't bother him. They just skeev me out. I just don't understand what their deal is."

Rob looks back over at them but they are gone.

"If you see them again, let me know and I'll get Rick on it. I know you don't like him but sometimes it pays to have friends who are cops. He owes me one anyway. I'll sic him on them and they won't be a problem ever again."

"Alright. Let's just get going so I can stop thinking about them. They friggin' creep me out," Anne replies.

They continue their walk up the sidewalk as Anne adjusts the hat on Gabrielle's head. They come across a small antique store and Anne's eyes fill with excitement. She skips over to one of the windows.

"Ok Hon, try to keep an open mind. This is what I wanted to show you. Come here and check this out."

He looks to the sky and mopes over to the window to peer in.

"What am I looking at?" he asks.

"Come on. I asked you to have an open mind."

"Ok, ok. What is it?" he asks again.

"What do you think about that table set over there for the dining room? I saw it a couple of weeks ago and I just love it. What do you think?"

Rob stares at the set for a moment and is about to speak when from around the side of the building, Krieger appears.

"Well, 'ello miss."

Startled, Anne reels around staggering back into Rob.

"What do you want with me?"

Rob steps up. "Something I can help you with pal?"

153

Krieger smiles and answers, "Naw, just enjoying this warm day and saying 'ello to my fellow town folk."

"Rob, this is the loser who feels the constant need to be an asshole whenever he can," Anne utters.

"Now, that's no way for a lady to talk, now is it? Think about the children," Krieger mockingly states while pointing to Gabrielle.

"'Ow's your friend the Professor? Seen much of him lately?"

"I haven't seen him in months. Now, will you please leave me alone or I'm gonna call the cops," Anne shouts.

Robs gets in Krieger's face and states, "Or maybe you and I can take care of this somewhere?"

Krieger looks up at Rob who is taller than he, then over at Anne and Gabrielle.

"Nah, we're good. Besides, I wouldn't want to ruin the baby's day out." Krieger pauses as he looks up at Rob. "Nor your pretty face, eh lad."

He displays an annoying smirk as he retreats backwards down the alleyway. He keeps a wary eye on Rob. When he's far enough away, Krieger shouts, "Tell the Professor we'll be keeping tabs on him, too."

Rob counters with, "Whatever, jackass." He turns his attention back to Anne.

"How long did you say this has been going on?"

"For a while now. I forget about them, and then a week or so goes by and they'll pop up again somewhere. He hasn't done anything to me. They'll just pass by somewhere and he'll make some smart-ass comment and then they disappear. He's never threatened me and he always has those two idiots with him. They

154

never say a word. They're just there. They and the whole damn situation is creepy."

"Well, I'm giving Rick a call as soon as we get home and that'll be the end of it."

"Yeah, you're right. This really has gone on long enough. Thanks, Hon."

Rob, sensing that Anne is still shaken up by the encounter, attempts to change the mood.

"And as for the table set. Let's go check it out."

Anne smiles at him as he opens the door for her. The three enter the shop but as they walk in, Anne looks one last time toward the alleyway wondering how the Professor could be linked to these men and why they have continued to hound her.

# SUPPORT

Monday night after work, Rob pulls his old Nissan Pathfinder into the driveway. He decided to leave work a little early so he could pick up some groceries that Anne had mentioned they needed.

Still suspecting she might be a little upset about the weekend's encounter, he figures this would be a good opportunity to give her a break. Ideally, he would like her to sip some wine and chill out for the evening. Meanwhile he will take care of dinner and put Gabrielle to bed.

As he rounds the final corner on his street before reaching his house, he sees an unusual and familiar vehicle a little ways ahead. It is the unmistakable taillights of Professor Caerwyn's 1969 Jaguar, but where it's going is quite puzzling to Rob. The Professor is making a left hand turn into Jack's driveway across the street.

Rob slows as he nears his own driveway and tries to look up Jack's driveway with little success. Jack's entire front yard is surrounded by tall, thick, very well-manicured bushes. Jack's driveway is also long and winding, making it impossible to see much further than ten yards.

Curious but ultimately uninterested, Rob pulls into his own driveway and parks his little SUV.

With groceries in hand, he catches a glimpse of Anne on the phone through one of the side windows. He rounds the corner onto the back deck. From there, he can clearly see that she is crying and obviously very upset. Just short of the door, he focuses on her and trying to hear the conversation but it is pointless. He can't hear a thing, so he just stands there and watches her as she talks. Unaware of Rob's presence, Anne concludes her conversation with the unknown caller.

"I know, I know. I just don't know how to have that conversation," she pauses.

"Fine. If you think it is best, I'll try. Ok, goodbye."

She hangs up the phone and wipes her face with a dishtowel.

Rob, obviously concerned and eager to find out what is troubling his wife enters through the door on the deck leading him into the kitchen. He quickly drops the bags on the center island and hurries to her side.

"Hey, hey. What's up?" he asks.

Anne does her best to hide her emotions and puts on her best face to Rob.

"Oh, nothing. That was Christina. We just have some girl stuff that we're working through. Nothing you should concern yourself with. We'll be over it and back to normal in a couple of days."

"You sure? I've never seen you this upset over a little cat fight."

Now suddenly pissed, she spins towards him and yells "Rob!"

"Alright, alright. Just a girl thing. If you wanna talk about it, you know I'm here to listen."

He pulls some groceries from the bags and starts putting them away. He looks at her with an annoyed expression. She doesn't acknowledge him as she also takes some of the groceries out of the bags to put them away.

After several minutes of silence, Anne puts both hands down flat on the island and begins to sob.

He moves behind her and grabs her shoulders.

"Anne, what's wrong? Tell me."

She shakes her head then turns to him and buries her head into his chest.

She begins to mutter, "I didn't know how to tell you because I knew you would be upset, but you have to know."

"Anne, I'm sure we can figure it out. Just tell me. Please?" he pleads.

She releases from him and takes an emotional step back while looking to the ground.

"Ok, you really wanna know? This is it."

She raises her head and looks at Rob's concerned expression.

"That wasn't Christine that I just got off the phone with. It was Dr. Shinto and he had some news that is going to be difficult for you to hear. I know because I can't believe it myself."

"What?" Rob asks getting increasingly frantic.

"He said we can't have any more children."

"What? How is that possible? What happened?"

"I've been to see him a bunch of times. At first, everything seemed normal. But then, I was concerned that I hadn't had a period yet. Every time we met, we did the same two sets of tests. One of them was six weeks after Gabby was born, a couple visits in between, and another a few days ago. In all instances, Dr. Shinto saw a drastic decrease in my estrogen levels. Like nothing he has ever seen before in a person my age. In the last test, they were so low the only conclusion he could come up with is that for some strange reason I'm menopausal."

Rob's silence conveyed a lot to Anne. She knew his brain was taking it all in and trying to find a rational solution but his expression said it all. He didn't have one.

"Anne, that doesn't make any sense. You're only 27. He has to have made a mistake. What about a second opinion? He just must've over looked something."

She looked up at him again and calmly stated what she knew.

"Rob, we checked everything. There are two critical hormones. The first is my FSH levels, which were way up and they shouldn't be. And the second is my estradiol levels, which are way down. There is absolutely no explanation for it."

Shocked and in disbelief, Rob smacks his fists down on the table with disgust.

"Anne, there has to be a reason."

"Rob," she interrupts "Listen to me!" she shouts.

She calmly places a hand on his arm and stares solemnly into his eyes.

"Honey, the last test we did confirmed it. I've stopped ovulating. I won't be able to have any more kids."

episode on so many months ago. She takes a seat, and as her body nestles into the cushions, she begins to examine the unusual book.

Leafing through it, her eyes begin to widen but her brow crumples with confusion. Much of what she had originally written is there but there is more, much, much more than what she and the Professor had drafted. There was page after page of new content that she had never seen before. Growing ever more confused, she flipped to the chapter she and the Professor entitled, The Basic Principles of the Kingdom.

Again, she finds most of her writings are there but there is a great deal more that was added. It is this new information that she finds striking. Some of the new entries read, "The basic rules of being a lycan are simple. Once a seasonal change, before the equinox or solstice, the wolf must willingly feed on live kill. If a lycan does not feed, on the next full moon after the $21^{st}$ of the month, the subject will succumb to the curse and change to wolf form. While in wolf form, the subject will hunt and kill. After such an incident has occurred, the subject generally has no recollection of the event."

She flips through to another page which reads, "Subjects can transform into human, wolf or lycan form."

"Subjects cannot transform in the sunlight. However, it is possible to transform indoors, underground, or in well-shaded areas."

"Subjects are not immortal but some individuals have been documented to live as long as 700 hundred years. Because of this unique trait, Kingdom members are expected to have prominent careers which will allow them to contribute to the Kingdom's financial stability."

Anne feverishly leafs through more pages but she spies one quick blurb that stops her dead.

It reads, "Female subjects can only give birth to one offspring."

Paralyzed with disbelief she slams the book shut.

Anne's mind grows anxious as a thousand questions race through it. The problem is, there is nothing she can grasp onto that makes any sense.

Overwhelmed with emotion, her eyes well up and tears streak down her face. She re-opens the book and attempts to try and find answers to her questions.

While she frantically flips through more pages, a large warm hand gently touches her left shoulder. Surprised, Anne lets out a quick yelp as she whips around to see that the Professor has entered the room. She looks up at him with tears in her eyes and her mouth wide open. She tries to speak but no sound emerges.

The Professor breaks the silence.

"Anne, you were never meant to see that. But now that you have, things have changed and you and your family could be in danger."

Still looking up, sobbing she asks, "Professor, what is this book? Is this fiction? This can't be real. This is a fictitious book right?"

"Anne, my dear, this-" slowly grabbing the book from her, "is a history book. It is one hundred percent factual and unfortunately now that you have seen it, there are some things I must share with you."

The Professor's face is grim but still calming. He walks around the couch and takes a seat on the other couch that is facing her. He rests his elbows on his knees and his chin on his hands. He leans slightly towards her and begins to speak.

"Anne, this book is a history book commissioned by the Kingdom and all the other major werewolf clans around the world. All the warring clans settled on a momentary truce while it was being written so that collaboration between the clans would be possible. Do you remember those scrolls and books that we had here for research?"

She shakes her head in affirmation.

"Well, they all contributed them. They did this so there would be an accurate timeline of their history, founders and of the conditions that are involved in being a lycan. You helped write the foundation which is the copy you possess, but when we were done I went back and added in and changed some of that foundation to make it relative for lycans. That is the book that you hold in your hands."

"After that, they were printed up and delivered to Kingdom leaders and the senior figures of the other wolf regimes. They did this for several reasons. One is so they can have an accurate history, one that can be passed down through their generations. Or, they can use it for recruiting new blood into their clans and to help people newly initiated into the lycan world. There are rules that they'll need to live by now that they are lycans. This book will help teach them."

Anne murmurs a question.

"Professor Caerwyn, are you part of this? This lycan, werewolf, whatever world?"

The Professor looks solemnly at Anne. He stands up and walks to a corner of the library and picks up a modest sized wooden case. He brings it back and places it on the coffee table in front of Anne. He sits back down beside her. He opens up the case exposing its contents to her.

He stares back at her puzzled face.

"Anne, we are all part of the lycan world."

# CONFRONTATION

After a stressful day at work, Rob arrives home and is surprised to see the Professor's Jaguar in the driveway.

"Aw shit, what now," he blurts out loud.

As he gets out of his car he almost trips over the shovel he purposely left out this morning to remind him to borrow Leon's hedge trimmers for this weekend. He quickly glances over to Leon's garage and can see the light on and faint movement.

*Great, he's in the garage, I can ask him right now,* Rob thinks to himself. He opens the wooden gate separating the neighbor's yards and heads over to the door on the side of Leon's garage. When he gets close to the window he can see that Leon is polishing a sword. And not just any sword. A large sword, way too big for him to handle. Rob stops in his tracks.

"What the hell," he quietly whispers to himself.

Never recalling a conversation with Leon that would indicate he was an antiquities collector, Rob further investigates the scene. There are also huge daggers and what appear to be light armor lying on the table in front of him. What's really odd is that everything there seemed too big for human use. After all the strange things that have happened in the last few weeks, this was the weirdest.

Not quite as odd was the cabinet open behind Leon that housed all nature of guns, from pistols to shotguns. They are all neatly displayed with boxes and boxes of ammo organized below. Another little tidbit that he had never shared with Rob. He did have a military background, so maybe this isn't that unusual, but definitely worth asking about.

Leon kept on polishing the sword with a rag when suddenly Stephanie walks in behind him with an armload of clips, fully loaded, and ready for use. She lays the clips down on the table beside Leon and spreads them out.

Suddenly, as if sensing him, she snaps her head up to see Rob standing outside the window. Leon too quickly looks up to see him.

There is a brief moment of uncomfortableness as Rob's face begins to feel flush when Stephanie quickly steps back and flips the garage light off. The garage goes black.

Completely embarrassed, Rob slowly turns around and walks back to his house.

Red faced and perplexed by the awkward situation he turns his focus to the next dilemma that awaits him at his house. Why is the Professor here?

He enters through the front door and Rob can hear both the Professor and Anne in the living room talking.

"Hello?" he shouts.

"We're in here," Anne replies.

Rob drops his bag on the counter in the kitchen and turns back toward the living room. He rounds the corner to see the Professor and his wife sitting on the couch.

"Ah, Robert, I'm glad you're here. Will you come in and join us? We have much to discuss."

The Professor stands to greet him which a gentleman's handshake. Rob obliges but senses immediately that the Professor's demeanor is very serious.

"Oh yeah, what's going on now?" Rob replies in an annoyed tone.

"Does this have to do with those three assholes Anne's been seeing around town?"

"Circumstances, Robert."

"Circumstances?" Rob replies.

"Yes, circumstances have suddenly changed and I'm here to discuss with you, your family's future."

"Circumstances. Future. What are you talking about? My future is of no concern of yours and I can assure you, if it were up to me, it wouldn't have anything to do with you at all. And why is it, whenever weird shit happens to my family, you're not far behind with a visit?"

Before the Professor can respond to any of the allegations, Rob abruptly ends the meeting.

"I think it's about time this relationship between you and my wife ended and I'll kindly ask you to leave, Professor?"

"Robert," the Professor abruptly shouts, "Sit down!"

The feeling in the room is tense but Rob eventually takes a seat next to his wife. The Professor continues. "You don't have the foggiest notion as to what this relationship is about and I believe it's about time you learned. There is an opportunity here for you and your family to have a more fulfilling life than you could ever imagine. Let me ask you, wouldn't you prefer to have more stability in life? Or would you like to continue on, the way you have been, by just getting by?"

The question sends Rob into a fit. He gets up and moves face to face with the Professor. The Professor surprisingly doesn't flinch at Rob's advance and this noticeably surprises Rob.

Anne, knowing how fiery her husband can get, stands up and gets between the two men. She looks at the Professor and says, "I'll handle this Professor. Would you please excuse us while we talk?"

"Certainly, my dear, but please," he glares solemnly into her eyes, "Time is wasting."

He steps back, still staring at Rob. "We'll talk later, my boy."

He puts on his hat and walks out the front door. Minutes later the sound of his E-type is heard starting up and backing out of the driveway.

The whole scene puzzles Rob.

"You know, Anne. That must be one helluva book."

"What are you talking about," she inquires.

"Well, it's been how long and you're still getting enormous checks every month. I've done some checking. I've looked in bookstores, online, and even on the NY top seller list and it's nowhere to be found.

So who's buying it? And just what the hell about our future do we have to talk about with him?"

"Well, part of what we need to discuss is the money," she calmly responds.

"Ok, that's good for starters. What about the money?"

Anne pauses, "The money that we get every month, is not from the book's sales."

"What? Where is it coming from?" he snaps.

"It's coming from the Professor."

"What?" Rob pauses and harshly glares at Anne, "Why the hell is he sending us money?"

"He's been sending money so that I could stay at home and spend more time with the baby."

Anne looks at the floor briefly, tearing up again. She looks back up at Rob who suddenly sees that she is growing more upset by the moment.

"And until you can calm down, that is all I'm going to say about it."

She turns and runs upstairs.

"Hey wait, Anne," he hollers.

She slams the door to the bedroom.

The sudden commotion wakes Gabrielle and she starts to cry. Rob's shoulders drop and he begrudgingly walks up the stairs to the baby's room. He picks her up from her crib and tries to calm her down. Almost instantly, Rob's mood improves as holding Gabrielle always has a calming affect over him.

Rob cradles the back of her head and tries to soothe the upset child. Gabrielle, within just a few moments of being with her father, stops crying. Rob continues to comfort her with his calming voice and firm hold until she eventually falls back to sleep in his arms.

The bond between father and daughter is something that is unique and only the two understand its true significance. It's difficult to put into words unless you've experienced it personally, and unless you're a man, you can't identify with it.

The bond between mother and daughter has been well documented throughout the years but the relationship that daughters have with their dads is sometimes more unique. A wink or a nod that leads to an unspoken understanding. Although not always said, a daughter has complete cognizance of protection and trustworthiness that only her father can deliver. This comfort level that they each share with one another is a bond that is very difficult to break, even sometimes under the direst of circumstances.

# REVELATION

The past week was a trying one for the couple but today is Saturday and the town is abuzz with students and tourists. The shops and cafés are full and the day couldn't be more beautiful. A delicate, warm breeze caresses everyone under a bright blue sky. After lunch Anne joins her neighbors, Jack and Louise, for a trip downtown to do some afternoon shopping and squeeze in a visit to Rob who is trying to catch up on some work at his studio today.

After the short trip to town, Jack maneuvers his Chevy Tahoe into a parking lot and snags one of the few available spaces. The couple exits the vehicle. Anne unbuckles Gabrielle from her car seat while Jack opens the back of the truck to retrieve her stroller. He clicks a few buttons and it pops open. He wheels it over to Anne who is pulling her daughter from the car seat.

"Thanks, Jack."

"No problem, my little lady," he replies.

Anne grabs her shoulder bag and with that, the four head towards Main Street where all the familiar shops and cafés can be found.

They get to the center of town and Anne decides she would like to share an ice cream with her daughter before the hectic shopping begins.

She loves ice cream and will get it at every opportunity. Fortunately for her, her daughter shares the same fondness for ice cream.

"Guys, I'm going to go get Gabrielle an ice cream. Can I get you two anything?" she asks.

Louise is first to respond, "You're sweet, I'm all set and unless he's considering going up a pants size today, he doesn't need anything either."

Jack rolls his eyes. Louise catches him and quickly elbows him.

"Ok, then. We'll meet you two over by The Gap in 10 minutes."

"Ok, but don't be too long though, they're having a big blowout on those shirts Rob likes," he adds.

"We won't, Jack. See you in a bit and save me anything you think he might want."

"Will do," he says with a smile.

Anne and Gabrielle leave the couple and make their way over towards the ice cream shop. She orders up a cone and hands the counter person a five. Anne collects her change and tosses it into the tip jar. She wheels the stroller over to a vacant bench and sits down to share the ice cream with her daughter. Gabrielle immediately grabs at the cone and attacks the ice cream with her mouth. The toddler, almost on command, has it all over her nose and cheeks. Her mother giggles and is right there with a napkin to clean the young one up.

The two finish their treat and Anne wipes everything down with baby wipes. Once cleaned, she stands up and is startled to be face to face with an unknown stranger. It is Beauregard and he has been quietly standing there observing Anne with his typical serene expression. She steps back and quickly looks the gentleman over.

"Oh, excuse me. I didn't see you there," she states.

She glances down again and notices he is holding a copy of The Kingdom. Only his doesn't look like the one the Professor gave to her, it looks just like the one the Professor has.

"Pardon me. You must be Anne? I've heard so much about you and from what I've read, it turns out that what I've heard is all true."

She looks at him awkwardly.

"I'm sorry?" she asks.

"About your writing, my dear," he states, holding up the book so she can see it. "You truly have a gift. My name is Beauregard Ramses. I'm one of the contributors to this read. I must say that you and the Professor have done a bang up job."

"Oh, oh! Why thank you Mr. Ramses," she says surprised.

"Call me Beauregard. I feel like I practically know you from all that the Professor has told me. That's why I'm here in town to meet with him and catch up on some old business."

Anne feels awkward around her new acquaintance and is having a hard time looking him in the eye. Louise, who was frantically scouring through clothes racks, stops when she notices that Anne is talking to an unusual guest. Visibly anxious, she grabs Jack by the arm and motions for him to look through the front window of the store at Anne. They both keep a watchful eye on the meeting as they hurriedly make their way out of the store towards them.

"I don't know what to say. I'm flattered. It was a pleasure working with the Professor, not to mention the astonishing subject matter," a modest Anne continues.

"Yes, well you did a great job and unfortunately, as luck would have it, I must be off.

Before I leave though, who is this precious little thing?" gesturing towards Gabrielle.

"Oh, excuse me, this is my daughter Gabrielle."

"Gabrielle. Ah, what a pretty name. Do you know what it means?"

He bends down on one knee in which to observe the young child better.

"Yes. The Professor told us."

"Of course he did. Such a beautiful girl. I love the smell of babies, don't you?" he asks.

He leans closer toward Gabrielle and plays with her hands. He closes his eyes and smells the top of the baby's head. His smile withers.

His eyes suddenly open wide as he stares down at the child. He seems noticeably angered but tries to mask his emotions.

"She smells like roses. Such a sweet thing," he mutters.

Anne's neighbors yell from across the street as they run towards them.

"Beauregard! Get away from that baby!"

He stands quickly, scowling at Jack and Louise as they insert themselves between him and Gabrielle. He is even more angered by their meddling and backs away from them. He looks back at Anne in disgust.

"My dear, it was extremely telling to meet you but I fear I'm late for my meeting. If you'll excuse me."

He spins and jogs across the street and continues his hurried pace down the sidewalk.

Anne is quite confused by Beauregard's irritation as well as his sudden departure. The three continue to watch him as he fumbles in his overcoat looking for his cell phone. Visibly agitated, he finally digs it from his pocket and frantically dials.

He quickly places the phone to his ear as Krieger picks up on the other end.

"'Ello"

"We must move now. The girl, find out where she lives. We are putting the plan into effect immediately."

Jack and Louise continue to watch Beauregard as he walks away shouting on the phone. He eventually disappears from view as he rounds a distant corner. They look at one another as they simultaneously pull out their cell phones and also start dialing.

"Louise, what's going on? Why did he get so angry? How do you know him?"

Anne is getting very nervous.

Louise takes the phone from her ear and peers into Anne's eyes.

"Anne, sweetheart, listen to me very carefully. Run, don't walk, to Rob's. Get him to leave work, get your truck, and come back here immediately. We'll watch Gabby. Now go!"

Anne, aghast by Louise's request pauses momentarily.

"Go!" Louise yells.

# RACE HOME

Anne is sprinting down the sidewalk. Her lungs struggle to maintain her aggressive pace as she pushes herself to reach Rob's shop. When she finally reaches his studio, she violently flings the door open. The bells on the door wildly jangle as she rushes in. In between deep gasps for breath, she manages to shout to her husband.

"Rob!"

He comes rushing out from the back room.

"What! What's going on? Why are you out of breath?"

"You have to come with me now. It's an emergency!"

"What is it? Is it Gabrielle? Where is she?" he frantically asks.

"Yes, just come on!" she urges.

Rob looks over at his co-worker.

"You ok to close up Pete?" he asks.

"Yeah, yeah of course. Get out of here," Pete replies.

Rob leads Anne out through the back door to the parking lot behind the shop. They hurry through the lot to find their truck in a sea of vehicles.

"This way, it's over here," he beckons. They each rush over to each side of the SUV as Rob struggles to pull his keys from his jeans.

"Rob, you have to hurry!" Anne shouts.

"Ok, I'm moving!"

He hits the button on his keychain unlocking the doors. They both jump in and Rob starts up the truck. With a flick of the gear lever, he tears out of the parking lot.

"Head over to the public parking lot. That's where she is," Anne instructs.

"Is she ok?" Rob asks.

Anne fails to respond. Her mind is racing at the moment and she doesn't hear him.

"Anne, is she ok?" he asks in a louder tone.

"Yes, yes she is!" she shouts.

She attempts to temper her emotions as she looks directly at him and pleads in the calmest voice she can muster.

"Will you just please hurry?"

Rob feels helpless as he desperately maneuvers the little Nissan down the road towards the public lot. When he pulls into the entrance of the public lot he spies Louise waving her arms at them. He pulls up in front of the couple. Louise hurries over to them carrying Gabrielle. Jack opens the back door while Louise puts the baby in her car seat. Once she is clicked in, Jack goes up to Rob's window to give him instructions.

"Now listen to me very carefully, Rob. I want you to break every speed limit and get home. We'll follow you. Whatever happens, whatever you see behind you, ignore it. You must get home. Lock Gabrielle in the basement and wait for help."

"She looks fine, what's going on?"

"Rob!" Jack shouts demanding his attention.

"Listen to me. Drive now! Get home. Do you understand?"

Jack is glaring intensely at Rob.

"Yes, I'm going."

"Good, now go! And don't stop, no matter what you see!" Jack yells.

Rob pulls out of the parking lot and accelerates down the main drag towards home.

Jack runs back to his Tahoe where Louise is waiting. He pulls out onto Main Street with his tires squealing, barely avoiding several pedestrians crossing the street. The commotion is enough to turn heads in the busy downtown.

When they reach the edge of town Rob looks over at Anne.

"Anne what the hell is going on? One, why am I speeding? I can't afford a ticket right now. And two, why do we have to lock our daughter in the basement? She looks fine."

Anne, upset and scared, looks back at Gabrielle, then out the rear window. For the moment, all she sees is Jack's Tahoe.

She takes a deep breath to calm her nerves long enough so she can talk to Rob.

"Rob, this is one of the things that the Professor and I needed to talk to you about. It's very complicated to explain right now but all I can say is that Gabrielle is in danger and we need to protect her."

"In danger? From who?"

"Rob, please. Just drive and trust me. I'll explain everything when we get home. Please, I'm begging you."

Tears well up in her eyes and drip down her face. Reluctantly, all he can do is trust his wife right now.

"Fine," he concedes, "But this seems a little beyond paranoid."

Anne turns back to watch out the rear window. The two vehicles are cruising around 60 mph on roads posted at 35. Both Rob and Jack use the entire road to maneuver the tight twisty turns. All is clear for a while but when they get a few miles out of town, two vehicles quickly appear behind Jack's truck. One is an old Ford pick-up truck while the other is a retired Crown Vic police car. The Crown Vic is still painted in the familiar black and white paint scheme but doesn't have any of the lettering or lights it once had. The Vic rolls up fast behind Jack. It is about to ram him when Jack slams on the brakes and the Vic disappears under the back of the Chevy. The front end of the car is crushed and the headlights explode into a shower of glass.

The old Ford uses the opportunity to get by. It pulls around and tries to accelerate past, but Jack matches its speed and sideswipes the backend of the truck causing it to skid off the road. It slides sideways about a hundred feet and eventually comes to a halt, stalled on the shoulder of the road. The driver starts it back up and hits the gas. The tires spin and a cloud of dust pours from the rear wheels as it races off to continue the chase.

Rob does his best to keep up the pace but two more vehicles have joined the chase behind them. They are high-powered BMW sedans. Jack swerves from side to side ramming the vehicles and preventing them from getting past. His Tahoe is slowed from trying to fend off the previous two vehicles. The embattled SUV has taken a fair share of damage but Jack pushes it on.

He persists with his defensive driving trying to give the young couple time to escape. The Vic, front end crushed but still running, tries to pass Jack again. He swerves hard, crushing the front corner of the car and causing the tire to blow. The car veers off the road as the driver locks up the brakes. The tires screech and a plume of white smoke follows it as it sails off the road into the woods.

Louise yells in celebration but is cut short when the pickup rams the Tahoe hard from behind. Both Jack and Louise's heads snap hard against their headrests from the impact. The BMWs fly past on the left while the Ford takes the opportunity to pull along the opposite side. Undaunted, Louise reaches in her purse for a black 9mm pistol. She swings her arm quickly out her open window and rapidly empties the entire clip into the cab of the truck. The hail of gunfire causes the driver to lock the brakes and dive back behind the SUV. Louise wastes no time ejecting the clip and snapping in another. She takes aim through the rear window at the beleaguered Ford.

"Cover your ears, honey!" she yells.

Jack takes his free hand and presses his ear closest to her. She holds the back of her seat with her left hand and takes aim with the pistol in her right. She pulls the trigger in rapid succession again. The rear window of the Tahoe shatters as thousands of pieces of glass shower down on the road. Bullet holes appear in the windshield of the Ford and the driver swerves back across the road to avoid the barrage of bullets.

Further up the road, Rob notices that Leon's Ford Expedition is parked on a side of the road up ahead.

"Anne, is that Leon right there?"

Anne turns to look as they pass the vehicle.

"Yes it is, thank god!"

Rob looks at her in dismay.

Leon accelerates out from the side road and pulls in behind the couples Nissan. He positions himself to take on the rapidly approaching BMWs that have evaded Jack.

Leon pushes a button and the rear window descends into the tailgate. Steph has positioned herself in the back with an arsenal of shotguns and high caliber pistols. The BMWs close in on them and Steph instantly unloads everything she has on the oncoming vehicles. She steadies herself as she fires a round from her 12 gauge at the closest BMW. Part of the hood buckles and the windshield explodes. She pumps, reloads, and blasts another shot, this time aiming for the front tire. The shot misses the tire but hits the headlight causing it to explode. The BMW swerves violently to avoid being hit again. Both BMWs dart back and forth very quickly trying to draw fire but also avoid being shot. After emptying the shotgun, Steph throws it down and grabs one of the sidearms.

Fortunately, Steph is wearing ear protection, because when she unloads the gun's clip into the front of the BMW behind them, the sound is like cannon fire. She manages to inflict some major damage as the BMW's front tire explodes. The car slows to a halt. Its radiator split and spewing steam while the driver's side of the car rests on bare rims.

"Nice work, baby! Keep it up!" Leon yells back.

Steph smiles at him and reaches for another shotgun. The other BMW falls way back awaiting reinforcements.

Rob has been catching glimpses of the fracas going on behind them while he skillfully maneuvers the roads towards their house.

"I don't know what you've gotten us into Anne, but this is crazy!" he shouts.

He pushes the Nissan hard around corners and practically gets it sideways while turning onto their road.

Their neighbors eventually disappear from sight and no other pursuit cars are seen from that point on. Rob quickly looks from Anne, to the road, and then back over at Anne but says nothing.

They finally pull up to their house to once again see the Professor's E-Type parked on the road beside their driveway.

"Oh, how convenient for him to be here. I should have known," Rob states.

The Professor is, however, nowhere to be seen. Rob comes to a screeching halt in the driveway. He leaps out of the truck then snags Gabrielle from the back seat. The three of them run into the house. Anne heads down to the basement with Gabrielle while Rob locks the front door.

"Lock everything," she yells up to Rob as she herself locks the bulkhead doors.

She comes back up the stairs.

She avoids his obvious frustrated glare as she closes the basement door behind her and locks it shut with a click of the handle.

"Where did you put her," he asks.

"I wrapped her up tight and put her in the spare crib down in the laundry room."

"Well great, she should be safe there. Now, you wanna tell me what the hell is going on?" he sarcastically shouts.

"Rob, what time is it?"

"What time is it? Who gives a shit what time it is? What's going on?" he demands.

"Rob! What time is it?"

"Fuck!" he yells.

He looks at his watch and replies, "It's quarter to four, why?"

"They'll be coming soon, help me lock all the windows and doors."

"From who," he shouts. "Who is coming here?"

"Rob, there is an organization that wants your daughter dead. Can you please help me secure the house so I can explain it to you?"

"Jesus Christ. This is bullshit!"

He storms off to the kitchen to lock the patio door. He then slides the kitchen window down and locks the top. He stops for a moment and hears Anne running from room to room upstairs. He is absolutely beside himself and can't believe what he is witnessing.

"How the hell did our neighbors get involved in this?" he shouts up to Anne.

There is no reply.

She comes down the stairs but she and Rob both freeze when they hear a sound. A sound that is unusual for this part of the country. It is also very close. It is the sound of a wolf howl. A lone single howl.

Anne whispers to herself. "Oh shit."

She hurries down the stairs and enters into the kitchen where Rob is. She looks at him and they both are about to speak but are interrupted by another howl. There is a moment of eerie silence that is broken by many, many more howls.

Rob turns his head away from Anne and looks out the big sliding glass door.

"What the fuck is that?" he demands.

He turns back to Anne who has the look of terror on her now very pale face.

"Oh my God," she whispers. "They're already here."

# ESCALATION

Two white vans speed along the road leading to Anne and Rob's house. Coming around the final corner, they maintain their speed until they are just at the couple's home. The first van skids to a stop in the driveway while the other stops beside the Professor's Jag. The side door of the first van slides open and six very disreputable men from Krieger's clan step out. Their clothes are dirty and they are brandishing various swords and daggers.

Looking around and surveying the house, they then look back to their leader, sitting in the driver's seat, for direction. He gives them a nod and four of them split up along both sides of the house towards the back. The remaining two look around, cautiously surveying the situation as they monitor the front door.

The second van and its occupants wait cautiously by the road.

The sound of vehicles driving at high speeds alerts all of them to take notice up the road to see what's approaching.

What they see are four large SUVs roaring over the crest of the road heading toward the house. The first two vehicles are Jack and Leon's and they look as though they've been through a demolition derby.

Jack's embattled Tahoe leads the way with a steady stream of white smoke pouring from the engine bay. He careens his truck head on into the driveway aiming for the lead van. The two intruders guarding the door fail to avoid the oncoming disaster as they are collected on the front of Jack's bumper and crushed into the side of the van.

The collision is sensational as pieces of glass and shards of plastic explode from the impact. The van is sent flying through the hedges, flipping onto its side and eventually landing in Leon's driveway.

When the Tahoe settles to a stop, Jack checks on his wife.

"Are you ok?"

"Yeah, I'm fine," she says.

"Good, let's go."

The two exit the vehicle and jog to the end of the drive.

Leon and Steph come to a skidding halt in the middle of the street followed closely by two more vehicles that appear to be with them. Leon steps out of his Ford, and from the behind the seat he pulls a massive steel sword that Rob saw him polishing nights before. It looks medieval and is way too big for him to handle.

Steph jumps out of the rear window still brandishing a 9mm handgun. She quickly unloads the 14 round clip into the remaining white van as she hustles around to meet her husband. The occupants scatter out of the van doing their best to avoid the bullet storm.

Leon leans his sword against the truck and pulls out three more swords from the back seat. He hands one to his wife and the other two to his neighbors.

The newcomers in the remaining SUVs, who have now parked behind Leon's Ford, hustle over to join them. Most are carrying remarkable looking swords while others strap oversized leather collars around their necks adorned with long spikes.

Jack grabs at the front of his button down shirt and pulls it apart sending buttons flying into the air. Underneath he reveals an oversized brown leather chest plate with a very familiar crest on the front. It is the crest of the Kingdom. The entire group follows suit and begin to remove their jackets and shirts, revealing the same chest armor as Jacks, making known where their allegiances lie.

The intruders from the vans now see that these are members of the Kingdom and begin to take action. They too begin to arm themselves with swords and knives. They also follow suit by removing their tattered clothing showing chest plates with the crest of Krieger's clan.

Fortunately for the combatants it isn't quite summer yet, so the days are still somewhat short. As the Kingdom members look intensely at the intruders, the sun is beginning to disappear behind the tall trees. Sunset has begun. Long shadows from the trees cover the driveway and stretch into the street.

Like a bell had just gone off at a boxing ring, the two factions swiftly change into lycan form. Their heads expand as their limbs extend beyond normal measure. Hair bursts out of pores all over their bodies and muscles bulk out. Bodies grow to towering heights, completely filling out the once loose fitting chest plates.

They now stand almost seven feet tall and their snouts extend out. Their human teeth are replaced with rows of larger more intimidating wolf teeth. Once completely transformed, they hold their weapons ready for action. The once giant sized swords no longer look so huge in the hands of these massive combatants.

The members who had attached the leather collars change into wolves. The spiked collars prevent any would be attackers from biting down around their throats.

Jack lets out a howl, like a signal, inviting others to attack. Louise snarls as the group advance towards Krieger's men.

The rival clan members prepare for the attack.

The two clans face off in the driveway for a battle of epic proportions, one that has not been seen in over a hundred years.

Lycans from both sides tear off what's left of their seemingly primitive human clothes revealing various clan crests and different styles of armors to protect each warrior in battle. There is a broad collection of weaponry being used, each chosen by its owner to best suit their combat style. Everything from massive broad swords, close combat daggers, or medieval style maces.

With the blink of an eye, the two sides storm at one another in a savage brawl. Swords strike one another with a high pitch metallic clang. Daggers pierce flesh and blood pours from wounds. The battle quickly spills onto the lawn. Huge paws dig into earth as these massive beasts push into one another trying to gain leverage.

More vehicles from both armies arrive. Cars crash through the fence skidding to a stop on the lawn, all while expelling more lycans to join the mêlée. Additional warriors come pouring out of the surrounding woods.

The battle spreads out all over the property. These rival clans from centuries past are battling one another, punching, biting, and savagely trying to tear flesh and limbs from their enemy. More of Krieger and Beauregard's people arrive, both on foot and in vehicles, as do members of the Kingdom. Swords and daggers continue to clang and clash as dismembered torsos from both sides drop to the battlefield in defeat.

The scene is bloody and primeval. Hundreds of combatants are engaging each other all over the couple's property. Giant lycan beasts slash at one another with weapons from centuries past. Powerful claws tear at opponents. Others who have taken wolf form speedily dart all about, lunging at the throats of their enemies and trying to dig their paws deep into flesh. Packs of wolves bare their teeth and snap their powerful jaws at each other. Others can be seen running into the woods given chase by packs of larger more powerful wolves.

The war for the Kingdom has begun.

# INTRUDERS

**B**arricaded in their home, Anne and Rob struggle with the reality of what is occurring beyond their walls. The scene outside is one of utter chaos. Rob has been glued to a tiny window in the hallway watching the amazing events unfolding outside. Anne hurriedly retrieves a large leather case from the hall closet, which distracts him momentarily. Curious, he follows her into the next room. She places the case on the kitchen table and opens it up. Inside, lay an assortment of guns and exotic looking silver daggers.

Rob looks at her in amazement and asks, "Where the hell did you get those?"

"No time for that right now. Just take them," she yells.

She quickly hands him a weapon for each hand. A dagger and a pistol. Outside a large crash is heard accompanied by a snarl and yelping. Robs hustles back over to the small window to investigate. There he witnesses violent skirmishes everywhere.

"Holy shit! I can't believe what I am seeing," he yells.

Warriors from Krieger's clan are hurled into trashcans, which cause a barrage of thunderous crashes. Other lawn furniture is smashed and broken under the goliaths' powerful steps.

"I hope those guns are loaded with silver bullets," he shouts half joking.

"Don't worry, they are," Anne replies frantically.

Rob snaps a look at her in disbelief.

Just then, three wolves crash through a giant picture window in the living room. Glass nuggets shower the floor as the wolves land on the couch under the window. Under the force of their landing and their immense weight, the couch collapses. When it does, the wolves lose their footing and stagger to the floor.

The lead wolf rights himself as the other two untangle themselves from the furniture they have destroyed. They survey their surroundings, carefully avoiding the broken glass scattered across the floor. The wolves eventually spot the couple in the kitchen. They growl with a threatening snarl and slowly advance toward the helpless duo.

Abruptly, the front door explodes off its frame. The heavy door falls to the floor with a crash as splinters of wood scatter down the hallway. Inns, in lycan form, steps over the door as he enters the house. As the wolves had done, he too looks around and spies the couple in the next room. Krieger, in human form, steps out from behind Inns and also enters. The two walk down the short hall towards the kitchen. Inns steps to the side in front of the basement door as Krieger confronts the couple.

"You!" Rob yells.

"Ha, ha. Yes, me. Where is the little one?" he demands.

"You can't have her!" Anne screams.

She raises one of the pistols and quickly fires off three rounds at the lead wolf in the living room. It takes two shots in the chest as it rears back with a yelp and then drops to the ground dead. A shocked Rob gathers his wits enough to empty his clip at the other two wolves. His aim is precise, as the array of bullets hit the remaining wolves in various points on their torso. They yelp in pain as each bullet strikes them. They are dead before they know it. Their limp bodies drop to the floor with a thump.

Angered by this assault, Krieger swiftly changes to lycan form and both he and Inns charge at Rob and Anne. They plow into the defenseless couple. The force of impact knocks them back onto the ground and unfortunately causes them to drop their respective weapons which go skittering across the room. Without hesitation, the lycans hurry over, pick up the hapless couple and throw them across the room. They each crash hard into walls, leaving dents in the sheetrock. Before they can gather their senses, the two lycans rush over and pick them up again. They throw the dazed couple again back across the room into the opposite wall. Rob flies into the kitchen cabinets and drops to the ground with debris all about him. He looks up to see Anne lying on her side writhing in pain from her assault. A large hole in the wall above her shows where she hit while sheetrock dust slowly floats down all around her.

"I can do this all day, Laddie. Now tell me where the girl is," Krieger asks.

"No, I won't" Rob states defiantly while shaking his head.

"Ok, 'ave it your way," Krieger snickers.

The lycans approach the couple again.

Meanwhile, outside, Beauregard pulls his BMW into the driveway. He turns the car off as he looks out the window to see Jack's Tahoe with two of Krieger's warriors dead on the hood.

"Hmm," he mumbles to himself.

He opens the door and calmly steps out. Despite the carnage going on around him, he remains unflustered as he clicks a button on his key-fob to lock the car. Two wolves from his clan run up to him and sit like obedient, well-trained dogs awaiting orders. With a flick of his right hand, he sends them into the house to find the infant. The wolves turn and dart towards the front door.

They enter the house, wildly sniffing for Gabrielle. They make it to the end of the hallway next to the basement door where they detect the scent they are looking for. They scratch at the door and yelp to get the lycans attention.

Inns, who is holding Rob down by the throat, turns to see what the two wolves have discovered. He stands up and effortlessly heaves Rob into the living room. Rob collides hard into a bookcase.

Inns walks towards the basement door. Stunned, Rob rolls onto his hands and knees. He lifts his head to see that his tormentor is heading towards the basement door.

"No!" he screams.

Adrenaline kicks in as Rob shows no fear while trying to protect his daughter's life. He gets up and sprints towards the lycan.

He charges at Inns and hits him with all his remaining strength. The blow is hard enough to topple the enormous beast to the floor. In one continuous motion, he grabs one of the daggers lying nearby on the floor, turns and thrusts it deep into the downed lycan's back. Inns roars in pain and reacts by arching his back.

The beast flips around and flails wildly trying to pull the dagger from his back but no avail. He lets out a garbled roar and falls to the floor. Rob stabs at Inns repeatedly until he is convinced the lycan is dead.

Blood spills from the wounds. It drips down the course brown hair and forms a pool around the lycan. Rob turns his attention to his beleaguered wife, just in time to witness something astonishing.

Krieger, who is holding Anne in air by her throat, turns his head for a split second to check on his downed comrade, Inns. Now with Krieger's attention elsewhere, Anne turns her head to Rob and silently mouths the words "I'm sorry."

She turns back to Krieger, clenches her teeth and the most unbelievable event occurs.

The fine hair on her fair arms grows wildly. Her thin legs elongate and muscles bulk out to double their size. Rob stands in amazement as his once beautiful bride takes on the form of one of these hideous beasts. Her once loose fitting sweatshirt is now tight almost to the point of tearing. Overwhelmed by everything, he hasn't the strength to remain standing. He drops to his knees with his eyes fixed on Anne. His jaw drops.

Krieger, noticing the sudden added weight of his captive and girth of her neck, turns back to see that he is no longer holding the frail frame of a human but now the menacing bulk of a lycan. She growls and snaps at his face. Surprised, the veteran warrior stumbles back as she takes to the offensive by driving her head into his chest. She plows forward, driving him hard into the wall behind.

Rob, still in shock and unaware of his surroundings, becomes a victim of Inns. The dying lycan musters up a last bit of strength to dive at Rob. He lands close enough to grab Rob's arm and pull him downward. The lycan quickly snaps his jaws, just catching Rob in the shoulder with his sharp teeth.

Rob screams at the searing pain and elbows his assailant off of him. His adrenaline spikes again and he stabs the ailing lycan with the dagger several more times, this time assuredly killing his foe.

Rob refocuses on the fight between Krieger and his wife. They exchange powerful blows, knocking each other down and laying waste to their surroundings.

Rob grabs a nearby dishtowel and holds it to his shoulder. Cringing in pain he suddenly hears a deep throaty growl coming from behind him. He turns around toward the basement, back to where the two wolves were. The basement door, however, is now open and guarded by only one of the wolves.

The wolf eyes Rob coldly. Its menacing snarl warns Rob to keep his distance all the while refusing to move from its defensive spot. Rob quickly realizes the dire circumstance his daughter might be in.

"Gabrielle!" he screams.

Unexpectedly, a huge crash and yelping is heard coming from the basement. The combatants all freeze at the sound of the commotion downstairs and look to the basement doorway. The basement lights go out just after another huge crash shakes the floor. Then there is a quick loud yelp followed by nothing but silence.

The wolf guarding the door turns away from Rob to look down the stairway. It quickly ducks its head down narrowly avoiding the lifeless body of his accomplice flying past and smashing into the wall behind. The wolf drops to the floor where it lies limp and dead.

Startled, the remaining wolf raises its head to peer down the basement steps. What it sees causes its tail to lower and tuck between its hind legs. Quickly overtaken with fear, it backs away from the door and retreats out of the house.

Slow, heavy footsteps are now heard coming up the basement stairs. Anne and Krieger's gaze are locked on the basement opening. Rob also stares at the darkness in the basement.

Seconds seem like an eternity, as the footsteps cause the floor to shake with each step. One after another, the steps grow louder. As whatever it is slowly nears the top of the stairway, the heavy breath of something big can now be heard. Rob's heart is pounding hard enough that his chest aches. He is terrified by the thought of what might emerge from out of the darkness.

Slowly a snout appears, glistening, as its nostrils flare with each powerful breath. Below that, a mouth, brimming with teeth that are as long as a man's finger and sharp as knives. The head is monstrous, covered in dark hair, topping a body that is equally as gigantic.

The impressive lycan breaches the cellar doorway. This lycan is noticeably larger than the others, standing well over seven feet and is a fearsome sight.

Across its broad chest is a black polished chest plate with the gold insignia of his Kingdom adorning it.

The uniqueness of the armor can mean only one thing. The Wolf King is here.

Once at the top of the stairs, the King surveys all the broken furniture and scattered glass everywhere. Rob is in front of him, still kneeling, frozen in fear. The King turns his giant head to see Krieger, still grappling with Anne in the living room.

"Krieger!" he shouts in the deep, throaty tones only a lycan can achieve.

Krieger looks at him and growls angrily. He pushes Anne aside and charges at the Wolf King. The two embrace in a ferocious heavyweight-wrestling match. The lycan leaders attempt to drive one another backwards. Their claws dig deep into the hard wood floor. The wood splinters under their nails as each other is driven backwards. The whole time, Beauregard is silently watching the fight through a side window.

Anne gets up and quickly goes about gathering as many of the weapons scattered around the room she can find.

She converts back to human form and hurries over to Rob, who is clutching his injured shoulder in pain.

Krieger snaps his powerful jaws at the King, who counters by grabbing at Krieger's throat in an attempt to hold him back. This gives Krieger the opportunity to land a few blows to the King's side. His claws pierce the King's skin. The King counters with a ferocious swipe across Krieger's face. Blood seeps from the wounds and flows into his eyes, momentarily blinding him.

The Wolf King drives Krieger back against a wall and delivers a flurry of powerful blows to the head of his adversary. Stunned, Krieger falls to his knees, barely conscious from the onslaught. The King picks him up and heaves the lycan leader through the broken picture window.

The giant turns and approaches the couple. Blood gushes from several wounds at his side. He kneels down to inspect the couple when Rob goes after him with a dagger. Anne grabs his arm.

" No! He's here to help," she yells.

"He's here to help? Who is He? And where is Gabrielle?" Rob asks.

The Wolf King answers in his low guttural voice.

"She's still in the basement. Are you alright?"

"I think so. It stings a bit but I'll be alright."

Rob stares in disbelief at both the lycan and his wife. His nerves are shot and he just breaks down.

"Would somebody friggin' tell me why I'm talking to a werewolf? And why the hell is my wife a werewolf? Just what the hell is going on?"

Rob stands up and walks over to the sliding glass door overlooking the deck. He looks beyond the deck into the yard.

"And for the love of God, why is there world war three going on in my back yard? Somebody answer me!" he demands.

Anne lowers her head in disgrace and the Wolf King stands.

"Rob, now is not the time. I need you to focus on your daughter. This will be over soon. Then you will know everything. But your first priority right now is to protect Gabrielle."

The mood is suddenly broken when Christina of all people shows up at the front door.

"Annie, Rob, are you in here?" she yells.

She looks down at Inn's lifeless body on the floor. She quickly covers her mouth trying not to scream.

"Christina," Anne responds.

Christina steps over the body and runs into the kitchen but stops dead in her tracks at the sight of the Wolf King standing beside her friends. The King turns to her and growls. She screams in terror.

Anne steps up and puts her arms around the King to hold him in place.

"It's ok. She's ok. She's with us," Anne says softly.

She goes to Christina and gives her a hug.

"Anne, what is going on? What is all this? I saw you and Rob flying out of town so I got scared and followed. Then I saw all this and hid over in your neighbor's driveway. Once it seemed safe enough to come over I ran like hell."

"I'll explain it all later. Can you go downstairs and get Gabby? I need to take care of Rob's shoulder."

"Absolutely. Where is she?"

"She's downstairs, in the laundry room. I don't want her to be alone right now," Anne responds.

"Don't worry, I'm on it," Christina replies. She runs across the kitchen and down the basement stairs.

Anne turns back to tend Rob's shoulder. He just looks at her.

"Anne, enough of this. Answers! What is this all about? How is Gabby involved?" he pleads.

A couple of loud metallic crashes are heard coming from the basement.

Anne looks to the Wolf King.

"The bulkhead door!" she exclaims.

The King moves to look out into the back yard. He sees Christina running with Gabrielle in her arms and a pack of wolves around her, protecting her escape. He turns back to the couple.

"Your friend has betrayed you. She is not who she says she is. We must act quickly."

Rob gets up and rushes to the window. He scans across his backyard but is still in amazement at the battle being fought.

"There," the King points.

Rob eyes the pack of wolves running behind Christina and can see that they're heading directly for the woods. Rob's fears become reality when he sees his baby girl screaming in terror.

"I see her. They're taking her into the woods!" Rob yells.

The Wolf King notices several wolves and lycans from Beauregard's clan cutting from the battle and rushing after them. He rushes over to the other room and peers out the broken window to see that Krieger's body is gone.

He looks back to Rob.

"You must save her."

He hands the human a huge dagger.

"Go now! I will protect you the best I can. You must save the Princess!"

The Wolf King morphs into a wolf, jumps through the broken window and runs straight towards the forest.

"Princess?" he asks to Anne.

"Rob. Go. Save our daughter!" she pleads.

Rob looks at Anne with a horrified expression, and then jumps out the window after the King. He runs as fast as his body will allow, dodging battles and slain corpses. He tries his best to keep up but the Wolf King is already deep in the woods and out of sight by the time Rob even gets to the edge of the forest. A loud howl almost sounding like a battle cry emanates from the woods. Kingdom lycans and wolves stop to heed the rallying call. A large group of lycans breaks from their battles and race into the woods. The rest stay to continue the fight.

# BETRAYAL

The battle intensifies as wolves and lycans, fighting each other all over the property, dig deep within themselves to overcome their foes. Rob breaches the edge of the forest and hears Gabrielle's crying in the distance.

"Gabrielle!" he yells out.

Exhausted and hopeless, he keeps running until his lungs burn. Small branches whisk across his arms scratching his skin.

Struggling to maintain pace through the woods, Rob catches glimpses of wolves running not far from him amongst the dense ferns. They bark to one another in what seems to Rob to be an organized pursuit. Rob runs as fast as he can, hoping that should they attack, the Wolf King will be there to protect him.

Gabrielle's cries grow closer with every step he takes.

"Christina! Stop!" he screams in desperation.

The patter of paws approaching him quickly make him put his arms up for protection. The onslaught is suddenly stifled by a blunt collision ending with a quick yelp. Rob slows to a jog. He is exhausted. Snarls and fierce skirmishes erupt all around him. He can see wolves rear up and dive down upon their adversary with fangs glaring. Kingdom lycans finally arrive to stave off enemy wolves with axes and clubs. A powerful strike from a lycan on a wolf sends it flying. When it lands a few feet from Rob, he can see its skull is caved in. Nearby, a multitude of Kingdom wolves coordinate a precision attack to topple several enemy lycans. Two wolves go in and bite down on each of the lycans arms, then a third dives at his throat, toppling the beast down to the ground. Most of the warriors fall with an agonizing shriek. Their defeat punctuated by their silence.

Rob moves on to find Christina trying not to focus on his pursuers.

The sound of a creature running straight towards him stops him dead. He panics as he struggles to catch any sight of his attacker through the ferns. All around him are lush green ferns that are all waist high. In front of him, the ferns part as he finally sees the head of an oncoming wolf emerge from the sea of green.

Frozen in fear, Rob braces himself for the hit as the wolf leaps at him, baring its fangs for the attack. The Wolf King flashes out of nowhere tackling the wolf to the ground. He bites hard into the neck of the wolf and shakes violently from side to side. A final quick movement snaps his enemy's neck, killing the beast instantly.

It all happened so fast that Rob doesn't wait see the outcome. He just sprints away, calling for his daughter.

The Wolf King looks up to see Rob running off in the distance. Fearing he will be overrun, he lets out another long and powerful howl. More of his fellow compatriots hear the call and sprint into the woods to help their King.

After hearing the King's call for help, Christina and the wolves that were flanking her stop near a cluster of trees. The wolves turn back to confront the advancing threat while Christina stays behind to guard the child. She takes Gabrielle who is wrapped in a blanket and places her at the base of a large tree. She also turns and prepares to take on any foes that might arrive. She looks to the air and listens. She smells the air. She knows Rob is close.

Unaware of what her intentions are with the baby, Rob does his best to sneak below the ferns to catch her by surprise but to no avail.

"Come on out, Rob. I know you're here. I can smell you," she scoffs.

He waits patiently as she sniffs the air trying to pinpoint his location.

A skirmish breaks out very close to where they are and wolves can be heard growling and barking at one another. At the sudden commotion, Christina looks in the direction of the fight. Seeing this as an opportunity, Rob quickly lunges at her with dagger in hand.

She just barely catches a glimpse of him out of the corner of her eye and at the last second, she grabs his arm and flips him across her body. He lands out of the clearing, back into the ferns. Fortunately, the ground is soft and he is uninjured.

"Nice try Rob," she boasts. "I'm faster than you, stronger than you."

"And uglier, I suspect," he interrupts.

He stands up, revealing himself in the ferns and stares down Christina.

"Christina, what are you doing? You're Anne's best friend. What is this all about?"

"Oh, Robby," she giggles. "You truly have no idea the magnitude of what you are involved in, do you? But you can't blame yourself or Anne. It was by chance that we became friends, her and I. But when she started working with the Professor, my superiors told me to investigate her further. I truly do love her and you for that matter, but what's at stake is bigger than all of us. You are caught right in the middle of a war for power and wealth of which you can't even fathom."

He brushes ferns aside as he enters the clearing where she stands defiantly between him and Gabrielle.

"And your wife is the Queen of it all."

"What?"

"You really don't know?"

"You lie!" he shouts.

"I do? Well, you can witness the beginning of the end. All I have to do is kill your daughter and that will set the wheels in motion for our victory!"

"No, don't!" he yells. "I'm begging you. Don't kill my baby," he sobs.

"You're such an idiot. It's not even your baby!" she laughs Christina drops to all fours and changes into a wolf.

Again, Rob is astounded by what he is witnessing.

"Is there anyone I know who isn't one of you fuckers?" he shouts.

Christina looks at Rob and bares her fangs. She then turns and approaches Gabrielle.

"No!" Rob yells.

He runs and dives at the wolf managing to wrap his arms around the beast's midsection and tackle it to the ground. Christina swiftly snaps her head to attack but as she does, Rob thrusts the silver dagger hard into her side. The wolf yelps loudly several times as Rob pushes it deeper. He quickly swings over on top of her, raises the dagger high above his head. Christina quickly converts back to human form.

"Rob don't," she begs putting her hand up in defense, her other hand grasping at her wound.

"You aren't going to kill me. Look at all we've been through. You can't."

Rob pauses as he stares at his wife's best friend. Her naked body is filthy. Blood is trickling through her hand. She clutches her side and Rob does start to feel remorse about her situation. But then Gabrielle cries from her location by the tree. They both look toward the child and then back at one another. He sees the deceit in Christina's eyes. He rears back with the dagger and drives another devastating blow into her chest.

"No!" she screams.

She changes into a lycan and snaps at Rob with her long pointed fangs. He struggles to hold the dagger with both hands. He musters the last bit of strength he can and with all his might, twists the dagger.

Christina lets out a bloodcurdling howl that slowly fades to silence. Her body goes limp and she ceases breathing.

Rob exhales a huge breath and crawls over to his screaming daughter. He picks her up and cradles the frantic child close to his chest. He pats her on the back and hushes her to stop crying. All around, battles still rage on but lucky for Rob, none of them are in his immediate vicinity. They also seem to be subsiding.

Finally calm, Gabrielle feels comfort in her father's arms. Holding her head in his arms and rocking her from side to side, Rob looks up into the early evening sky almost sobbing.

A lycan steps out from behind a tree. It is Krieger.

"Well, well, well," he says in his deep raspy tone.

Rob whips around quickly to face the giant lycan. He pulls the dagger from Christina's chest and points it at Krieger.

"Stay away from us you son of a bitch!" he shouts.

"Why? What are you gonna do, Daddy?" Krieger asks in a sarcastic tone as he raises his giant broadsword to compare it to the dagger. "Mine's bigga'," he boasts.

He reaches out with his hand towards Rob.

"It appears that with one strike of me claw the Kingdom will be one step closer to being mine."

He lets out a vicious snarl and lunges for Rob and Gabrielle.

Another lycan leaps from the vegetation and tackles Krieger hard. It is the Wolf King. He has cuts all over his head and arms. His once beautiful armor is battle scarred and covered in blood and dirt. They both fall awkwardly to the ground. The Wolf King lands on a sharp root that pierces through his leg.

Krieger steadies himself and goes for another lunge at Rob when, from out of nowhere, he is seized by the throat. Yet another giant lycan, the size of the Wolf King reveals himself. He is as large but with much lighter fur and his armor is polished brightly with colored rubies encrusted in the crest. He stands tall holding Krieger high in the air by his throat. Krieger attempts to pry the huge claw from his throat but has little success. This lycan is too powerful.

It is Beauregard.

He stands tall, holding Krieger high off his haunches as he utters a final statement to him.

"I'm sorry Krieger but your kind will never take the throne. Your people are good for one thing and that is fighting. You do it well but the next wolf king will be of a more elevated stature, not a peon like yourself."

Krieger tries to turn his head to face Beauregard but the lycan leader tightens his grip around Krieger's throat. He grabs at Beauregard's arms and kicks his feet to no avail.

He slams Krieger against a tree. Krieger leans back against the tree trying to free himself from Beauregard's grip but is too fazed from the impact to do so.

"So my friend, it's good to have goals."

Beauregard pulls a saber from a sheath at his side and thrusts it through Krieger's mid-section, impaling him to the tree.

Beauregard releases Krieger, whose body just hangs there on the sword. He leans over to get face to face with him and states. "Just make sure that they aren't too lofty."

Blood drips from the Krieger's mouth as his body goes limp.

Beauregard now turns his attention to Rob and Gabrielle.

"Well, to quote my good friend here, it appears that with one strike of *my* claw, the Kingdom's future will be one step closer to being mine."

The Wolf King, who is trying to free himself from the root, utters, "Beauregard, your fight is not with them. Take your fight to me. I'm the one you want."

"Not right now, your highness. I'll deal with you soon enough. You know as well as I, that if I kill you she is still heir to the throne. If I take care of her, then it'll be just you and me. And of the two of us right now, I think I can take ya."

"Beauregard, leave her!" the King growls.

"Your reign is over," Beauregard scoffs.

He pulls the sword from Krieger's lifeless body, and in doing so, it flops down to the ground.

"Now, Princess, prepare to die."

Beauregard aggressively advances toward Rob and Gabrielle with his sword raised over his head.

Rob shields his daughter with his body. Two blasts echo through the forest. Gabrielle is startled by the noise and starts crying again. Rob looks to see that Beauregard has unexpectedly stopped his approach and his eyes are wide with confusion.

His sword falls from his hand and stabs into the mossy ground next to him. Still stunned as to why he can't move, he drops down to one knee before the father and daughter. He stares coldly at them attempting to reach for them with his outstretched arms. Three more blasts are heard and Rob now recognizes the sound as gunshots. They hit Beauregard twice in the back and the third and final shot square to the back of his head. The clan leader hunches forward and falls to the ground.

As he drops, Rob sees Anne standing behind him holding a smoking pistol.

# DECISION

The battle carried on into the evening but with their leaders having fallen in battle, the remaining factions eventually abandoned the fight and retreated whence they came.

Now that the threats have subsided, Kingdom members congratulate each other and surround their injured King. The heroes of the battle make their way back toward the house. The sun has set and the forest is once again peaceful and quiet. The sounds of crickets replace the clanging of swords. Most of the warriors help their fellow comrades with dressings to their wounds. Others tend to the dead.

The Wolf King, Rob, Anne and Gabrielle exit the woods into the back yard. The yard looks a medieval battlefield. Shields and swords lie everywhere. Corpses of lycans and wolves are strewn about. The last few remaining wolves run off escaping into the woods. Leaderless pack members stand dazed as they ponder their fates. Kingdom members congregate in groups. Some mourning the loss of their fallen while others celebrate their victory.

Leon is standing on one foot while leaning on his wife. Rob looks to him and nods. He responds with a nod and a smile.

"Don't you worry about this. We'll get this cleaned up so it won't affect our property values one bit."

As the Wolf King makes his way past, all of the Kingdom's soldiers bow their heads or drop to a knee in respect to their leader. He responds to everyone with a nod or respectful hand praise. After he passes, they return to the task of collecting their weapons. The mammoth cleanup will take hours.

Inside the house, the Wolf King slowly transforms into his human form, which to Rob's astonishment turns out to be the Professor. Louise is there sweeping up all the debris. Jack is standing over by the island in the kitchen wrapping a bandage around his forearm.

Louise approaches Anne and offers to get Gabby cleaned up and bring her to her room upstairs. Anne hands her the exhausted child and says thank you to her neighbor.

The three of them sit on the battered couch in the living room. The Professor begins to tell Rob what has transpired here today.

"Rob, let me begin by saying that what you took part of today and how you dealt with the adversity is something that you should be very proud of."

"Professor, before you go on, what is all this, I mean, werewolves? What the fuck?"

"Lycans, Rob. We are an ancient civilization that has the capability to shape shift into human, wolf or lycan form. I am their King."

"You mean that the people that you and Anne wrote about in that book are really you?"

"Precisely," the Professor responds.

"OK, fine. But I still fail to see how this has anything to do with me or my family?"

"Rob, what I'm about to say, I am ashamed of. I hope though that my estimation of you is correct and you can understand the gravity of these facts. The truth is that Gabrielle is not your child."

"What? What are you saying?"

"What I'm saying, Robert, is that Gabrielle is my daughter and heir to my throne. You must understand Rob that I cannot take just anyone to bare my children. They must be exceptional, and Anne is that. Smart, young and courageous."

"You son of a bitch. How could you do this to me? How the hell do you expect me to take this? Positively? And you-" he turns to Anne, "How could you?"

"Rob, Rob, please. Don't blame her. She was an unknowing participant. She only just found out a few days ago. I can assure you that she was completely unaware of what was happening. As I said, it is not something I am proud of. But I did so that she could bare my child. She had no idea what was going on. Now please, if you can, let's put all that aside for a moment because you have a bigger responsibility to think about right now."

Steph walks into the living room and offers an armload of moist towels to the trio. The Professor accepts them and thanks her for her assistance. She then tends to the laceration on the Professors leg.

Anne takes one of the towels and wipes her face and arms with it, as does the Professor with his. He takes another one and places it on his wounded midsection.

He looks back at Rob and continues. "As I was saying, your wife and daughter are already part of the Kingdom. You've been bitten and soon you will become one of us. I have no desire to take Gabrielle away from you or break up your family. What I would like very much is for you and Anne to raise her. If you join us, your life can continue in any capacity you wish. You can continue to live here, you can travel the world or do whatever it is you choose. You can quite literally live like a king."

"What about all this? Will Gabrielle's life continually be threatened?"

"Yes. From time to time, factions will rise up and try to take control of the Kingdom. Your family will be well protected, just as you were today. Besides, with Beauregard and Krieger out of the way, there won't be anyone to get those rogue clans all fired up again. Those two were our biggest antagonists."

"Professor, you've been interfering in our lives pretty much since I met Anne. All those years of meddling has led to this. What's to say I just don't kill you once and for all?" Rob brandishes the gun that Anne shot Beauregard with. The others in the room get anxious at the situation and flare up to protect their King. He raises his hand to calm them and to back away. He takes a deep breath, pauses and looks to the floor. He raises his head to respond.

"You could certainly try."

He stares sorrowfully into Rob's eyes. "But I don't think you will. You see, one of the reasons I chose Anne was because of her affiliation with you. You are smart, strong, and you have a good sense about you.

That's the type of person I want raising the heir to my throne."

Rob stares at the Professor, drops his head, and drops the gun to the floor. Louise quickly grabs the weapon.

"I just don't know. Jesus Christ, this whole thing is just fucking unbelievable right now. How do you expect me to hear all this and just say *yeah, sure, why not? That would be swell.* I need some time to take all this in, and think with a clear head."

"Robert, I expect nothing less," the Professor replies.

Rob gets up off the couch.

"And Professor, my name is Rob. Only my parents call me Robert. Please respect that," he states and walks towards the stairs.

Anne gets up and grabs for his hand but he abruptly pulls it away and motions for her to stay away. He walks upstairs and enters the bathroom, closing the door behind him. He turns on the shower and cranks the temperature knob to hot. After a few minutes, steam starts to rise from the tub. Leaning on the sink, staring into the mirror, he notices his face is filthy with dirt from the forest floor. His arms are scratched and blood from his two lycan kills stain his clothes.

The steam from the shower slowly starts to obscure his image in the mirror. Taking a seat on the toilet, he begins the painful process of peeling his clothes off. The wound on his shoulder is amazingly already showing signs of healing.

He pulls the shower curtain aside and checks the water with his hand. One final adjustment of the knob and he steps in. Staring downward, Rob watches all the dirt and blood slide down his legs. It catches a stream of water flowing between his feet toward the drain and eventually circles down the drain. He doesn't move for twenty minutes.

After the prolonged shower, Rob dries off and goes to his bedroom to get dressed. Then he walks into Gabrielle's room. He takes a seat near her crib and watches her sleep. He loves her with all his might but is conflicted on how to feel, given the news that she is not his biological daughter.

After an hour, he returns to his bedroom, locks the door and takes a seat by a window overlooking the back yard. For hours he watches Kingdom members return his back yard from a battlefield to what is was before. Like a well-oiled machine, they clean up debris, gather weapons, and dispose of dead bodies. They haul away their dead for proper burial and burn the dead of the other clan members on sight. The fires burn all through the night.

Rob closes his eyes as his mind begins to drift. Gabrielle is not his child. His home life and family are not what he believed them to be. His family life has turned out to be a lie. His eyes grow heavy as the exhaustion of the day begins to settle in and he eventually nods off to sleep.

The morning sun breaks over the trees and shines into Rob's face. The bright sunshine awakens him from his slumber. The fires have extinguished themselves leaving bright orange embers sizzling in the morning dew. The ash circles emit a constant billow of smoke that snakes up into the sky.

He heads downstairs towards the kitchen and Anne comes up behind him.

"Honey, I'm sorry. I never wanted any of this. I promise you, I didn't know about any of this until a couple of weeks ago. I just didn't know how to tell you."

"I'm not blaming you. We just need to deal with it. We just need to deal with all this, somehow."

She looks down and notices that Rob is holding one of the pistols from the wooden chest.

"You wanna talk about that in your hand?" she asks.

"No," he abruptly replies.

"You know I'm here for you right?" she asks.

"I know. I think I'm gonna go for a little walk now before breakfast. I'll be back soon." he says solemnly.

"Rob, stay here and talk with me," she begs.

The Professor is lying on the couch with his leg tightly wrapped. He tosses back the blanket covering him and watches the confrontation closely.

Rob ignores her pleas and saunters out the back door onto the deck. He glides down the stairs from the deck into the yard. The remaining Kingdom members tending the fires nod their heads in respect for his valiant act of saving their heir's life. He respectfully nods back.

Anne watches him as he approaches the edge of the forest.

The Professor stands up from the couch and limps into the kitchen with the help of a cane that Louise had brought over for him. Anne's eyes well up and she turns to the Professor. He moves closer and wraps his arm around her to offer some measure of comfort.

"Professor, stop him! Don't let him go. Go after him, talk to him."

"Anne, have faith," the Professor states as he looks down towards Rob. His keen eyesight allows him to watch Rob until he disappears deep into the dense forest.

"Rob will make the right decision for him."

She pulls away and looks up to the Professor.

"No, no," she cries She pulls away and runs outside to the railing of the deck and shouts "Rob!"

"Rob!"

# ABOUT THE AUTHOR

Steve Szmyt was born on March 21st, 1971 in Methuen, Massachusetts. At a young age he moved to NH where he has been a lifelong resident. He graduated from Timberlane Regional High School in 1989. His collegiate studies revolved around graphic design and fine arts. In 1995 he graduated with high honors from Franklin Pierce College. On top of being an avid sci-fi fan his passions are music and art. He plays both piano and guitar with his 2 young daughters.

In 2002 his creative desires led him to start writing and since then he has many projects in various degrees of completion. He is keen to keeping his writing in an up tempo style that keeps the reader guessing and enthralled from the beginning of the story to the end.

Join the discussion at
https://www.facebook.com/Steven-Szmyt-265536550477532/
or on Twitter
https://mobile.twitter.com/Molyoy

CPSIA information can be obtained
at www.ICGtesting.com
Printed in the USA
BVOW04s1827160517
484301BV00001B/3/P